Whiskey Justice

Peter O'Mahoney

Also by Peter O'Mahoney:

The Bill Harvey Legal Thriller Series:

Will of Justice

The Max Harrison Legal Thriller Series
with Patrick Graham:

Criminal Justice

Defending the Innocent

The Paid Juror

Burning Justice

The Girl on the Road

Whiskey Justice: A Thriller

Peter O'Mahoney

The characters and events in this book are fictitious. Any similarity to real person, living or dead, is coincidental and not intended by the author.

This is a work of fiction. Any resemblance to any person, living or dead, is purely coincidental.

For Ethan, Chelsea, and Sophie.

Whiskey Justice

PI Tom Whiskey Book 1

1

Twenty years.

Twenty years since that beautiful face smiled at me. Twenty years since I last hugged her. Twenty years since I last held my little sister in my arms.

"It never gets easier, Tom," my youngest sibling, Andrew, rests his hand on my shoulder. "I still pray for her every day. I just hope that someone is up there listening."

We sit next to each other in the cold, empty church, listening to wind whistle through the gaps in the walls of the stone building. This church is where we spent a lot of our youth. This is where we spent every Sunday morning listening to an old man preach about a book he believed in. The day before my sister died was the last time I came to a Sunday church service. Since then, I have only ever stepped into the sacred walls for christenings, weddings, and funerals - the full circle of life.

As I sit in the front pew of the church, I hope that there is a heaven, and that my sister is up there playing with hair, singing songs in her angelic voice, and having a soda with my parents.

Out of my tattered wallet, I remove a small photo of her. It was taken the night she died.

It is the only physical photo I still carry with me. It might be old-fashioned, but I do not want to leave it behind. The photos of my cancer-ridden ex-wife, my drug addicted son, and my mentally unstable friends are all stored on my phone, but I have no digital photos of Molly. When she was alive, photos were rare and precious. Selfies hadn't even been invented yet. Molly would have loved selfies. I could imagine her hanging upside down on the world's tallest buildings just to take the perfect selfie.

The photo is as creased as any photo that has sat in a wallet for twenty years would be. Despite the age of digital everything, I will never stop carrying around this physical picture. Molly looks beautiful, smiling at the camera, with her long blond hair hanging over her shoulders. Her lovely gold necklace, the one that I gave her, rests around her neck. They never found the necklace. They said it must have been stolen after her death.

I should have been here for her.

I should have been able to protect her. She was my little sister, and I failed her.

Before she took her own life, I was in the Army, fighting a war that I didn't understand on the other side of the world. I arrived back two days before she died.

I should have been here for her.

"This place has sure lost its shine, Tom," Andrew says as he looks around the building. "I remember when it was full of life, and the seats were new, and the walls were spotless. Remember old Mrs. White? Her job was to clean the seats every week, and man, she took that job seriously. I remember I had to stand up during one whole church service because my butt was dirty with mud, and she wouldn't let me sit down." Andrew draws a long sigh. "But I guess people just don't come to church anymore."

"Do you?" I ask him.

"I bring the family once a year at Christmas time. I figured Mom and Dad would like that."

I nod.

My world is very different than the one that my younger brother belongs in. He sits next to me in his tailored suit, perfectly groomed, looking like a male model that has just stepped off a Milan catwalk. He is a lawyer, like our father was once, and like our deceased sister was trying to be.

I had taken different path.

I went to college to study law, but found the rules too restrictive. I jumped at the chance to join the Army and fight for my country. Little did I realize that the rules would be more restrictive there.

But it was an honor to stand next to the people I served with.

The people who stood beside me as bullets flew around us were the greatest men and women I have ever met.

Upon my sister's death, I became disillusioned with the establishment, and left the Army. I wasn't convinced that she had hanged herself. She couldn't have. Even today, I don't believe it. I just can't accept that a happy, carefree girl such as Molly would have taken her own life.

I tried to convince the police that it was a setup. I spent months arguing with them. But they didn't listen. Eventually, they threatened me with arrest if I didn't leave them alone.

I saw her the night she died, and she was as happy as she ever had been. There was no pain in her eyes. She had just booked an overseas trip with her best friend, and paid the money up-front. Why would she do that? Why wouldn't she even leave a suicide note? Those questions remain unanswered, even twenty years later.

"You're looking good, brother," Andrew says to me as I stare at the picture of Molly. "Your biceps look like they are the size of my thighs. Have you been working out?"

I laugh out loud. "What do you want, Andrew?"

"Nothing. I'm just saying that you are almost ripping out of that shirt."

I have always kept fit. My high school football coach told to me every day, 'When you are fit, you can do so much more with your life. You can live the life everyone wants.' I have never forgotten those words. "Andrew, in my line of work, physical fitness is a priority."

After I left the Army, I tried a number of office jobs, but none of them suited my aggressive personality. I was fired from six different jobs for swearing at the boss, swearing at arrogant customers, swearing at computers, and swearing at pens that wouldn't work when I needed them. When the opportunity came through to work for a private investigator, I jumped at the chance. Five years later, I started running my own practice.

I have been doing that ever since.

But people don't know I'm an investigator unless they come looking. I don't advertise. I don't promote. And I certainly don't brag. Word of mouth is the reason I get most of my business. And usually it is with people that can pay my very high fees.

"She will always be beautiful," Patrick Walker says as he looks around the church building. He runs his finger on the stone wall and grimaces at the picture of Jesus nailed to a cross. "I will always remember her as she was."

Patrick is my brother's best friend, and he knew my sister Molly well. They were dating at the time of her death, and he was torn up about the incident. Maybe that's why, after Molly's death, he became a New York City Police Detective… or maybe he did that because he is a power junkie.

Patrick Walker is also one of the most untrustworthy individuals I have ever met. I have the utmost respect for the men and women that work for the NYPD and risk their lives for the safety of the community, but for Patrick, I have none. He couldn't care less about his community. He only cares about himself. Patrick would steal a chocolate from the hand of a dying child.

Patrick Walker quit the police force two years ago to become a motivational speaker. He runs seminars, records YouTube videos, and takes money from people for yelling at them, and telling them to do better with their life. Apparently, there is a lot of money in convincing people that they are failures.

When my sister told me that she had started dating him, I almost spat out my drink. Even back then, I knew he was a creep. The worst type too. The type that disappears when it is his turn to buy a round at the bar.

"What's he doing here?" I turn to my brother.

"He said he wanted to pay his respects. They were dating when she died, remember?" Andrew says in a low voice. I don't care if Patrick hears me. He knows I don't like him. "He also said he wanted to ask you something."

"Of course," I say, shaking my head. "Always the opportunist."

"Do you like my new suit?" Andrew asks, as I place the picture of Molly back in my wallet.

"Always looking for my approval," I pat my shorter brother on the back as we walk out of the church. "It's a nice suit, but it wouldn't fit me."

Being six-foot-four, I have to get my suits tailored, not that I wear them often. My uniform is usually jeans and a black t-shirt, with a leather jacket if the temperature starts to drop.

"You're still the hero." Andrew stops and makes the sign of the cross as we exit the doors. "Everyone still looks up to Tom Whiskey."

"Literally," I add, as I rub the hair on top of his head.

After we walk out of the church into the cold New York City air, I gaze up to the midday sky.

"If there is somebody up there, please make sure that you look after Molly," I say, and I perform the sign of the cross on my body.

"I haven't seen you do that for a long time," Patrick smiles at me.

"It's in the hope that someone is listening," I nod. "I still feel like I failed her, Andrew. That feeling has never gone away. It's like a piece of me, now. Hopefully, someone up there is doing a better job than I did."

"Stop blaming yourself, Tom. It wasn't your fault. Molly wouldn't have wanted you to blame yourself; may she rest in peace." Andrew draws me into a hug before he opens the door of his car. I've never been much of a hugger, but Andrew is five years younger than me, and he loves to wear his emotions out in the open. "I'm due in court now, but I'll see you next week. You're coming around to my house for dinner, remember? No cancellations this time."

"I'll see what I can do."

"Sarah would be very disappointed if you didn't make it; so would my kids," Andrew says as he climbs into his new, large, shiny Audi. "And I'll see you tomorrow, Patrick."

Patrick draws a long breath as he stands next to me. "See you, Andrew."

I turn to Patrick, who has hands in his suit trouser pockets, waiting for Andrew to leave.

"What do you want, Patrick?" I question, looking down at the skinny man.

"Tom, I need your help."

"What do you want, Patrick?"

"I was robbed."

"You're a former NYPD Detective," I grin. "That's your job to sort that out. I'm sure they taught you a thing or two in the force."

He shrugs. "There's a problem, Tom. Some of the things that were stolen were to do with something illegal, and I can't be seen looking for them. If anyone found out it would be devastating for my career."

"Of course," I nod. "My fees are high, Patrick. And I raise my fees even higher when I have to deal with scum like you."

"I don't suppose you'll give me a discount for being your brother's best man?"

"No," I reply firmly.

"Ok, ok, Tom. I know you have never liked me, but I trust your professionalism and expertise. I trust that you can keep this quiet, and that's why I need you. If what was stolen got into the wrong hands, it could be very damaging for me and my family."

"So do you want me to recover the stolen goods or investigate?"

"Ideally, I want you to recover them."

I nod. "You need to pay me a very large retainer for my services – twenty-thousand up front."

Usually, I take a five-thousand-dollar deposit before I start a case, but with people like Patrick, I'll make that twenty.

"Of course," he nods. I know that he can afford to pay that money easily. "I'll bring the money, but my name can't come up with this at all. Do you understand? I can't be connected with this at all."

"My office, tomorrow morning at 10 o'clock. Be there with cash."

He nods, and I walk away.

When people make money quickly like Patrick has, they also make enemies. There will be people out to get Patrick, whether that is a competitor or someone he has stepped on along the way.

I have a feeling this case is going to be heavy.

And I like it like that.

2

New York City feels crazier today.

It is the full moon tonight and I can already feel the extra insanity on the streets. I walk past a couple of young adults arguing over Tinder profiles, a man talking to himself about the rats, and a preacher shouting at me to repent.

I watch as two sullen people walking down the street suddenly stop and smile perfectly, hold their pose for two seconds while they click the camera on their phone, and then return to their grumpy faces. Everyone is a model these days, perfecting their photos to show the world, but it is all so rehearsed. I wonder what those two people will see when they look back at their photos in ten years' time. Will they be convinced by their own perfect lies? Or will they remember the emotion of taking eight different shots to perfect the photo? Give me an awkward photo that reflects a beautiful moment any day. One of my favorite photos is a family photo that was taken the moment my brother's jumper caught fire from a nearby candle. Nothing can replace that moment. The photo is blurry, our faces aren't pretty, and none of us are looking at the camera. But when I see that photo, I remember my mother and father putting out the fire and my whole family, Molly included, laughing for the next week. That was a moment to remember.

But perfect photos are the way of life now, and I must either accept that and adapt or become a grumpy old man who tells well-worn stories about a forgotten time before smart phones.

As I trudge forward through the streets, amongst all the chaos, I see Greg Robbins, my old friend.

These days, Greg is unmedicated, homeless, and destitute, living in the subway, but he is still my friend. Through the rush of the busy Manhattan street, I lean down and sit on the sidewalk, next to the man who once saved my life. It is strange to see the world from this angle. Legs rush past us with determination. All of these people are walking somewhere, doing something, and having to be some place. And all I can see is their legs.

"Hello Greg," I say, as I toss a few green notes in his cup.

"Do I know you?" he asks with confusion.

He doesn't recognize me anymore. Post-traumatic-stress-syndrome hit Greg hard after Afghanistan. He was a good soldier, but never too smart. He graduated high school, but I think he was lucky to do that. Greg was an all-in, yee-haring, pranking solider. He was the happiest guy I knew. That was until he walked into a room full of dead Afghans after rebel gunfire. He saw murdered fathers, raped mothers, and mutilated children. That scene changed his life. His brain couldn't process what had happened. Nobody could process that.

Greg was never the same after that day, and his descent into madness was a slow and painful process to watch. We all tried to help him, but nothing could stop it.

He turned to alcohol and hard drugs when he returned home as he tried to suppress the memories of war. All that did was turn his mind to mush. At least he can't remember that scene anymore.

"We are old friends," I say to him. "How's life?"

"Couldn't be better," he smiles genuinely. "I have the three f's, and that is all I need."

"The three f's?" I ask.

"Yeah: Food, friends, and fashion."

"Ha!" I laugh out loud. It's good to see he hasn't lost his sense of humor. "Fashion?"

"That's right. Old, ripped jackets from the 80's are in right now. Just look at all the hipsters. They are all wearing what I wear. I'm a trendsetter!" he laughs.

"It's not my type of fashion," I smile.

"Hey, do you know the worst thing you can tell a homeless person?" he jokes, leaning close to me.

"No, I don't."

"Knock knock jokes," he laughs heartily. "We don't understand them!"

It's hard not to laugh with him.

His joy is infectious. Patting him on the shoulder, I smoothly slip fifty dollars into his coat pocket. He doesn't notice me do it. Hopefully, he will get a good surprise later.

“Enjoy your day,” I say as I leave my friend.

“You too, man. Thanks.”

“Don’t mention it. It’s only a couple of dollars,” I nod to his cup.

“Not for the money,” he smiles. “Thanks for taking the time to stop. It means the world to me that somebody stopped; more than you will ever know. Thanks, man.”

Filled with pride, I smile, nod, and then move on with my day.

And what a day it’s going to be.

When I arrive at my Manhattan office, Patrick Walker is already waiting for me. I nod to him and then to my assistant, the beautiful Kate Jones.

“Good morning, Tom,” Kate smiles. “You smell nice this morning.”

I put on an extra spray of cologne after I left Greg’s company this morning. He may be an old friend, but he could do with a shower. Or maybe eight showers. And then two cans of deodorant.

My smell has obviously caught Kate’s attention. “I always try to smell nice for you, Kate.”

“I bet you smell nice first thing in the mornings too,” she winks.

My heart skips a beat as she leans forward, exposing an ample amount of cleavage. I can't help but notice. That woman sure knows how to flirt.

Leaving my office door open as I enter, I invite Patrick to join me.

"Nice office, Tom," Patrick says, as he shuts the office door behind him. "Thanks for taking the case on. I know that you and I haven't always gotten along, but I have helped your brother a lot. Thank you."

"Don't jump the gun, Patrick. I haven't taken it on yet," I say, as I sit behind my large desk. "I've only agreed to look into it."

Patrick draws a long breath and sits down in the office chair on the opposite side of my table. He crosses one leg over the other, folds his arms, and looks at the 1997 Wayne Gretzky signed jersey I have hanging on my wall.

I love to read body language. It is something that interests me beyond a hobby. It's a passion of mine. The body conveys more than words ever will. You can talk the talk, but unless you walk the walk, I will see straight through it.

Patrick's closed body language is telling me that he is hiding something, and doesn't want to disclose it to anyone. I can imagine that coming to this office must be his last resort.

"I have to admit, Patrick, I am very intrigued," I say, as I lean backwards in my chair and drum my fingers on the edge of my large table. "So tell me more about this robbery."

"I tried to solve it myself. But… my job means that I have… restrictions," he shrugs. "If I dig in the wrong place, then this whole thing might blow up in my family's face. In this day of the internet, one wrong move can ruin entire careers. That's why I need someone not connected to my family to investigate. I need someone who is willing to get their hands dirty but not wash that dirt on me."

"What was stolen?" My question is direct. I have no time for people that want to dance around issues.

"A small safe."

"And what was in that safe?"

Again, he pauses before he responds. "It was a safe that is very valuable to me."

"Why?"

"You don't need to know that."

"I do," I respond firmly. "Let's get something straight from the start, Patrick. This is a private investigators office. This is not the police department. The rules that govern your old profession are different to the rules that govern me. If you want me to take on this case, then I need to know the details. All of them. If you don't tell me what's in that safe, then you can walk straight back out that door."

"Tom, you've got to understand that there is a high degree of discretion required; for me… and others."

"Who are the others?" My questions aren't open; they are more demands than queries.

Patrick shakes his head gently. He is trying hard to hold his secret from me.

"Kate," I punch a button on my desk phone, and calling my assistant. "Can you get us a confidentiality form?"

Within seconds, Kate sways into the office with the degree of confidence that comes with being very smart, blonde, tan, slim, and beautiful. "These ones?"

"Thank you, Kate," I say, as she walks back out of the room.

I toss a form in front of Patrick, and he scans it over. "This is just a form, Tom. A whole bunch of words. A form doesn't mean that you won't disclose the details."

"No," I shrug. "Still, I know that you old cops love a good form. It's an extra layer of security for you. If I disclose the details of your case without legal standing, I can be sued."

Patrick gently slides the form back across the table. "I want everything off the books. Payments, forms, details – nothing on the books. I don't want you to record anything on your computer, and I definitely don't want any emails or text messages about this. I don't want my signature on anything in this office. I can't be connected to you."

I drum my fingers on the table again, thinking over the situation. "You are going to have to tell me what is in that safe."

Patrick stares at me with his cold gray eyes. He's testing me. I don't flinch.

"Nineteen years ago," he begins, "I took evidence from the scene of a crime. The crime was never solved because of a lack of evidence. It has remained a cold case to this day. And I swore that I would never disclose that evidence to anyone."

"What happened?"

He takes another long pause.

"What happened, Patrick?" I press forward with my questioning.

"My father shot someone."

"Your father?" I ask in surprise.

"Yes."

Patrick's father is Thomas Walker, a well-known, high-ranking NYPD officer. He is the man that they wheel out in front of the television cameras every time that a cop needs to say something. He is the face of the NYPD.

Thomas Walker looks like a good cop. He looks like a great citizen who has dedicated his life to the improvement of the community. I have had the pleasure of spending time with Thomas Walker, and I know that he is a great man. His views are full of understanding, love, and tolerance – quite the opposite of his son. Thomas is known for his charity in the community, winning numerous awards and accolades for the work he has done for the homeless, the mentality ill, and the poor. He is a great man.

"Why would your father need to shoot anyone?"

"It was a long time ago, Tom. Nineteen years. It feels like a lifetime. My father shot the person in self-defense, but any investigation wouldn't have seen it that way. The contents of that safe will prove that he killed the person, and that would mean that his two decades of great work in the community would be washed away. I can't let that happen. I need that safe."

I have never liked Patrick. He has an intolerable sense of arrogance around him, and his attitudes are selfish and greedy, but I do like his father. His father has soft, welcoming eyes, and a warm soul.

"There's something I don't understand here, Patrick. Why hold onto evidence for the past nineteen years? Why not just throw it away? Dispose of it in a place where you know that nobody could find it?"

A sense of guilt washes over Patrick's face, "I should have. I really should have. I know that now. Hindsight is a wonderful thing. The fact that I held onto that evidence sounds ridiculous to me now. Of course, I should have disposed of the evidence. But…" he takes a long pause while he considers his next words. "There was a sense that I didn't trust that the evidence would never be recovered. I thought the safest place for it was with me."

"Like you were a protector of your family?"

He nods. "Like a protector of my father."

I understand that. Even if it made perfect logical sense to get rid of the evidence, there would have been an emotional element to the decision. It would have been his chance to feel like he had contributed his family.

That would have been hard to get rid of.

"What happened on the night that he shot someone?"

"I remember it clearly, Tom. Like it was yesterday. It was just after I had joined the police force and my confidence was through the roof. My father and I had watched a movie together, and we were walking back to the subway. I led my father down a dark alley, and I know now that it was a stupid decision. The second I stepped into that alley, I knew it was a stupid decision. But I was so full of bravado and confidence, nothing could touch me. And I wanted to take the shortcut. Really, I should have just walked around the block. It would have only taken five minutes extra to get to the subway. The shortcut wasn't worth saving the time."

"Or somebody's life."

Patrick sighs, "We walked down the alley, and someone tried to mug us. He was an older man who was quite weak. I don't know what he thought he was doing. He shouldn't have tried to mug us. So, he comes up to us, points the gun at my father, and demands his wallet. My father grabbed the gun from the man, and the man instantly surrendered. He threw up his arms in defeat. He said sorry to my father and even told him that he could keep the gun. But my father shot the man anyway. At point blank range. I knew at that point that I needed to cover that up. That piece of information could never escape to anyone. Nobody could ever know what happened that night. I checked the alley, and there were no witnesses. So I took the gun and we ran to the subway. And we agreed we would never speak about it again."

"Sounds like cold-blooded murder. That is not something that I am interested in defending."

"But look at the bigger picture, Tom. Look at everything my father has done for this city. You know what he has done. If it was to come out that he was a murderer, then all that good work is thrown out the window. That is not good for the community. Especially right now. The whole city is a knife-edge, and one little thing like this might tip the scales. We could see riots on the street if this gets out."

"Why did he shoot him?"

"To teach him a lesson."

"Death is a hard lesson to learn from," I reply sarcastically. "Who was murdered?"

"Does it matter?"

"To me, yes."

"Timothy was his first name. I remember the name because I watched that case closely for years. I made sure that it went cold."

"And so the contents of that safe would show your father's guilt?"

"Yes."

"Is that all that is in the safe?"

"There are some other personal artifacts in there. I don't even remember what is in there. Probably just some old junk, old pieces of memories. I haven't opened that safe in more than ten years. I had forgotten about it. It was just sitting in my cupboard for so long."

Patrick is my brother's best man. They grew up together – side by side through thick and thin. He saved my brother from a knife-wielding client once, and I have been indebted to Patrick ever since.

"And who do you think stole it?"

"There are two people that I would name as suspects. One – a girl named Jessica Watson. A nice, pretty girl, who does a lot of volunteering work, but, she is a thief. She was at my house last Wednesday talking to my wife. We have previously had things go missing when she was over. My wife even caught her going through our cupboards one time. Jessica is my wife's shift boss, so she has to be nice to her. They are both nurses, and Jessica has been to our house to discuss work timetables and swapping shifts. I'll give you her details."

"And suspect number two?"

Patrick draws another long deep breath, "Tan Do."

"The New Age priest?"

Patrick nods slowly.

Tan Do is a Vietnamese-born American priest who leads a New Age church called 'Heaven's Angels.' The church has eight branches throughout the US, but its head office is in NYC. It is an all-singing, all-clapping, rock music church that praises God with more novelty than tradition, but the people come to him in droves, looking for his blessing. Usually, he gives it as long as soon as he receives a sizable donation.

"And why would the priest want to steal something from you?"

"Because he is as dodgy as they come. You and I both know that. You've seen the grin on his face. He lives a very luxurious lifestyle for a priest. He was in my house last week as well. He came over for dinner two nights before I realized the safe was missing."

"Does he know your father?"

"He hates my father. He thinks my father steals all his spotlight. Tan Do just wants money and attention. If he could take my father out of the picture, he would."

"Doesn't sound very priest-like."

"You've met the man, Tom. You know that he isn't very priest-like. I probably have higher morals than he does."

"That's a low standard to be compared with," I scoff. "So, we have two main suspects?"

"That's right."

"Was anything else stolen that night?"

"Not that night. I thought Jessica Watson had stolen things before, but that was months ago."

Again, my fingers drum on my oakwood desk.

The rhythm of the movement is very comforting, and it enables me to think under pressure. I do my best thinking either drumming on a table, or whistling as I walk down the street.

Or in the bar with a few glasses of whiskey.

Whiskey always helps.

"I'll take the case, Patrick, but I am going to need to be very well-remunerated."

Patrick drops an envelope full of one-hundred-dollars notes on the table. "Whatever you want."

I nod.

That amount of money always helps me decide whether to take a case or not.

3

The first step in any investigation isn't to investigate the crime, the accused, or the circumstances surrounding the incident.

Nope. The first step in any investigation is to collect information about the person hiring the investigator.

Average, normal people with average, normal lives don't hire private investigators. People who are in trouble hire investigators. And that trouble means that they are likely to be hiding something.

Usually, what I find out about a client shapes the whole case.

Patrick Walker used to be a detective in downtown Manhattan, which means that finding information about him won't be hard. His life since he quit the police force has been a finely managed public relations exercise, and anyone that has met him in the last two years will have been conned by his confident persona. Over the past two years, his image has been crafted by social media posts, television appearances, and radio spots. His persona is so well rehearsed that there isn't a line that comes out of his mouth that isn't prepared.

I'm not interested in that Patrick Walker.

I'm interested in the Patrick Walker that stole money from the poor, beat up the innocent, and took bribes from the crooked.

On the first corner I visit in Brooklyn, on Vernon Ave, I see an old friend. And by 'old friend', I mean a person with whom I want nothing to do with, and is a drug-dealing snitch who will tell me anything I need to know for the right price.

"Taylor."

"Shit."

That's the usual reaction I get when I say hello to scum. My reputation precedes me.

The last time I saw Taylor Dean, I put him in hospital. He had given me information about an investigation I was doing, and I paid him well for his time. It was a mutually profitable deal.

But as a fourteen-year-old girl walked past us, he talked about getting her into bed.

I broke his jaw.

I didn't appreciate his comments.

He knows not to make those jokes around me now.

"Taylor, we are going to have a chat."

"Yeah, you're lucky I can talk after last time," he snaps back with attitude.

"You'll be lucky to talk to next time if you keep with that attitude." I feel like I am talking to a child. In some ways, I am.

Taylor Dean never finished high school and has been making his living on the streets since he was twelve. Dealing and stealing, his name is well-known on the streets. So far, he has avoided prison time by talking to the right people and giving information in return for safety. He has moved his drug-dealing operations from Queens, to Manhattan, and to Brooklyn in an attempt to escape local street thugs.

He is as versatile as he is crooked.

Part of me wishes that he did spend some time in prison - he could finish his high school diploma in there.

"Let's talk over here," he looks up and down the street before walking to the back of a beaten-up white van.

Taylor Dean casts a shadow over most people he meets. His clothes are a size too small, his beard is grubby, and his hair dangles over his wide shoulders. But Taylor Dean looks more like a rake than a telegraph pole. I don't think this man has eaten an ounce of protein in ten years.

I guess that happens when your diet is mostly white powder.

Taylor clunks the lock on the back door of the van, creaking the door open with a sound like fingernails on a blackboard. As soon as the door opens, I am hit with a waft of unwashed stench.

"You could do with some air freshener in there, Taylor," I comment.

"Can't smell much these days," he comments, sniffing like he has just done another line of crack.

Inside the old van is a dirty mattress, a pile of grimy clothes, a weighing scale, and a small locked safe. That must be where he keeps his drugs and money.

"Looks comfortable," I nod towards his bed.

"It does the job. The ladies love it."

"I think the term 'ladies' may be an overstatement, Taylor," I say.

"Ha, still funny old Tom Whiskey, eh? Yeah. They're not ladies; they're dirty whores."

I stare at Taylor with the look I gave him just before I broke his jaw last time.

"Or we can call them women if you like. Yeah, let's just call them women," he corrects himself in an attempt to avoid being struck again.

"That would be a good choice, Taylor."

"Welcome to my current residence, sir," Taylor says with a pretend posh English accent. "Please, sir, help yourself to a comfortable seat. We have only the best for the best at this place of business."

I nod.

As he closes the van door from the inside, I sit on a red plastic milk crate. It is not the most comfortable seat, but it is probably the cleanest item inside the van.

"I've got a joke for you, Tom. I've been waiting to tell you this one for a while," Taylor grins with joy.

"Go on," I humor him. "What's the joke?"

"What do you call an alligator in a vest?" he giggles.

"What?"

"An in-vest-igator!" he laughs hard. Harder than a man in his late twenties should laugh at that joke.

"I think I heard that joke in junior school."

"Ok, ok. How about this one?" he says, still laughing from his last joke. "It's not an investigator joke, but I like it." Taylor leans forward to me and says in a lower tone, "Who do you call when a swarm of mosquitos attack? The SWAT team! Hahaha!"

Taylor just about falls over laughing at the joke.

This guy is obviously high.

"Taylor, I need you to tell me everything you know about Patrick Walker," I stop him from telling any more bad jokes.

It takes him a while to stop giggling, and finally, he sighs, "You don't want to hear some more jokes? I've got a whole lot of them."

"Patrick Walker. What do you know?" I respond firmly.

"What's it worth to you, Tom? My time is valuable, you know. I'm a busy man. I have a business to run, and people to see. My time is valuable."

I put a ten-dollar bill in front of him. His eyes light up at the look of money. This man just loves money. He's addicted to gathering it, and he's addicted to wasting it on drugs.

"Double it, and I'll tell you everything I know."

Criminals are so easy. With educated people, you have to trick the information out of them. You have to outsmart them to make them say what you want them to say. But with men like Taylor, you just have to put the right price in front of them.

I lay another twenty down. Taylor nods.

"He's nasty. Real nasty. He's hit me up for information before. And by hit me up, I mean literally hit me up. Belted me around until I had blood coming out of everywhere. So I told him what I knew, and so he hit me again. Nasty. He's got a reputation around here for being crooked too. He will take money where he can, and will throw his power around. I wouldn't recommend becoming friends with him. He's not a good guy, Tom."

"I know that. But he's paying me well to investigate a case for him. So I need you to tell me what else you know."

"You know that he's no longer a cop? He's a motivational speaker now. Did you know that?"

I nod.

"Can you imagine that? A crooked cop becomes a motivational speaker? That's almost a joke in itself."

"I know about his current life, Taylor. I want to know about his past life."

"Alright. Well, he's got some friends on the streets that protect him as well. You know how it works. He protects the right people, and they make sure that they protect him in return.

I don't know what sort of business he is into, but I know it's not legit. If there is one guy that gives cops a bad name, it's Patrick Walker. He still comes down to Brooklyn a bit, I hear. He's a celebrity now, though. He can't do what he used to do."

"And what did he used to do?"

"Buy drugs."

"Are you sure of that?"

"Absolutely. And not just personal use, either. I'm talking large quantities. He used to purchase coke by the bucket. But I think he doesn't do that now that he is famous. He's still a regular at Stanwell's diner, which is two blocks that way," Taylor points down the road. "Ask there about him, and they will tell you the same thing."

"Who is Patrick connected to on the streets?"

"I heard that he was well-connected to the church."

"The church? That's not exactly a criminal organization that runs the streets."

"No, no," Taylor shakes his head. "Not the old church. One of the New Age ones. 'Heaven's Angels' church. It's all fancy, and singing, and full of money. The dodgy priest that runs the place sells more drugs than I do. He comes around to the homeless, pretends to help them, but really, he is just selling them drugs. He's got all sorts of people working for him too. He shouldn't be a priest. A Vietnamese guy. I don't know his name."

"Tan Do," I nod.

"Maybe. Like I said, I don't know his name. But I've heard that Patrick is connected with that church. That made the church untouchable for a while. And that's why I've never trusted the church. They are as bad as I am."

"That's not true," I state firmly. "The church is a great place for great people. But there are bad apples in every bunch."

"If you say so, man," Taylor shrugs.

"You should go to church, Taylor," I pat him on the shoulder and use my foot to push his van door open. "Confess your sins and say you're sorry. Maybe then you'll have a chance at going to heaven."

"If I had to confess all my sins, I'd be there a very long time, Tom!" He laughs as I walk away down the street.

I Google Stanwell's Diner on my phone to make sure I am heading in the right direction. Being a private investigator has changed so much in the last ten years. Technology has replaced a lot of local street knowledge. Once I had to do so much leg work, but now technology does a lot of that for me.

In a lot of easy cases, I can find out more from social media than I could have by asking around. I have solved cases within an hour thanks to the wonders of social media. Even criminals want to share their exploits with the world.

But technology still doesn't replace instinct.

Technology can never replace that moment when you look into someone's eyes and see a lie. It can never replace the feeling you have in your stomach when you know that a situation doesn't feel right. Technology can be programmed to tell a lie to everyone. If you program the system right, it can convince everyone of your lie. I quite often wonder about what would happen if the information sites on the Internet changed their data all at once. Would we all be convinced of their truth?

And that's why I will always have a job.

Stanwell's Diner is two blocks from where Taylor's van is parked, and I decide to walk as I need the time to think. It's a bad street in a bad part of town, but one of the benefits of being six-foot-four, broad, and confident, is that most people don't pick a fight with you. I can confidently walk down most streets and not feel threatened.

Stanwell's diner is what I expected. It isn't fancy.

In fact, it's probably the opposite of fancy.

The first 'S' on the sign is missing, indicating that this place might also double as a tanning salon. Once in the front doors of the diner, it would be hard to make that mistake. The place stinks of old coffee, burnt bacon, and cheap food. The benches are stained, the vinyl on the stools is frayed, and the till is a mess of papers, signs, and tip jars.

This is not a place I would usually frequent.

"What will it be?" a lady in her sixties yells at me from behind the counter, one hand on hip, cloth in the other. By the looks of these benches that cloth doesn't work that too well.

"Coffee," I give her a cheeky grin, and it instantly disarms her distrust for me.

She grins at me in the same way a grandmother grins at their cheeky four-year-old grandson. The woman takes a moment to select the cleanest mug from the shelf and then pours the coffee in there for me.

"I have a feeling you're not here for our famous coffee, young man," she winks as she places the coffee in front of me. That's the first time I have been called 'young man' in two decades. It's a surprise, but I like it.

"You are a clever woman," I say as I drop a twenty on the table. It's not my money. This will all go on Patrick's expense account under 'other working expenses.'

"That's not true," she laughs. "If I was clever, I wouldn't have been working in the same diner for the past thirty years."

"Thirty years? You must have started here when you were three years old."

"Ha!" she laughs heartily. "Flattery will get you everything."

"Good. I need to know about Patrick Walker," I say softly as I look inside the mug and see a piece of floating dirt in my coffee.

She nods and leans down on the counter. "He's a prick," she says firmly.

"I've met him," I smile. "I know that."

"Then there's not a lot else that I can tell you. He comes in here once a week, doesn't tip, and talks loudly on his phone. He thinks he is the president around here, just because he's a former cop. But he's not the president. Nobody likes him. To become president, you have to win the most votes."

"Sometimes," I reply.

"Patrick thinks he can bully people into doing what he wants. When he forgot his wallet and didn't have the money to pay for a mug of coffee last month, he said that he would shut this place down if I didn't give it to him for free. What could I do? The man is a former cop. He could walk in here, plant a bag of cocaine under the counter, and get his friends to arrest me. There was nothing I could do. Except, well, I spat in his coffee the next time he came here."

I'm not sure that would change the taste. "Do you know any of his connections?"

"Anyone who is dishonest has dealt with Detective Patrick Walker." She says his name with such disdain. "But I couldn't tell you the exact people. I could listen to his call next time and find out some names if you need me to. I'd be happy to see that man get into trouble."

"Maybe," I nod at her offer for assistance. "Is there anything else you can tell me?"

She thinks for a moment. "Yeah. There was a girl here asking about him last month. Cute girl, real friendly. She came in here, talked real nice to everyone, and then asked about Patrick. She wanted to know everything. I thought it was unusual, but like I said, most people would be happy for him to get into trouble."

"Did you catch her name?"

"Jessica."

"Jessica? Are you sure?"

"Yeah, it was Jessica. I'm sure."

Interesting.

"Thank you, beautiful. You have been more help than you could imagine," I stand to leave.

"You don't want to try our famous coffee?" she smiles.

"I've had too much coffee already today," I grin.

"I would leave it behind too," she mumbles to herself as I walk out the door.

Walking back onto to the street, I turn my jacket collar up to protect my neck against the fresh breeze. I've always thought that Patrick was a prick. And I haven't come across anything to dispute that opinion yet. That makes me uneasy.

If it weren't for Patrick's ties to my brother, I would walk away from this case now. I don't like helping criminals. I know that the line between good and bad can sometimes be blurred, but it's not in Patrick's case. He is a genuine prick. Selfish. Conceited. Arrogant. He's not the sort of person that I enjoy helping. The only thing that keeps me tied to the case is his connection with my family. That, and the money.

Although I earn a lot from my job, I also like to think that I am making a difference. As a private investigator, I help people. I make the world a better place.

However, with Patrick's file, I get the sense that it is not the case…

4

Whiskey always tastes good in this bar.

Actually, whiskey tastes good in any bar.

At any time of day.

There is something about the smell of good whiskey that tricks my brain into relaxing. I am sure that if I smelled a glass of whiskey, I could still feel relaxed while running late for a plane in LAX airport.

I'm sitting at my favorite bar on my favorite stool with my favorite drink. This is my place. A place where I feel comfortable to be me. The bar is full of old oak timber, clean but not sterile, charming and relaxed. The people are quiet, and there are no televisions, sports betting, or live bands here.

Just conversation when needed, and solitude when required.

Perfect.

"Try this," Dave, the bartender, places a second drink down in front of me.

"What is it?"

"Sullivans Cove French Oak Whiskey, voted the world's best single malt whiskey. Thoughts?"

I take a whiff, swirl the glass, and then a small sip. The taste hits me like a truck. That first sip always does. Once the kick dies down, the flavor washes through my mouth like a delicious, rich, and sweet river of love.

I nod my approval to Dave.

"I thought you would like it," he smiles.

Dave knows me as well as anyone. I have been pouring my soul out to him for the last ten years. He is an intelligent man, a great listener, and a thoughtful conversationalist. His musings have helped to solve some of my cases.

But, I once saw him outside the bar on the sidewalk in a different street. That was a weird experience. Saying hello to him on the street felt out of context.

"Good to see you, brother," a large hand rests on my shoulder. "This is the second time I have seen you in a month. That must be some sort of record for the past two decades."

My brother and I have always been close. We've had each other's back through thick and thin, but we don't see each other very much. Our lives have taken us different directions.

Andrew's life path has been by the book. He studied hard, got a good job, got married, had a child, got divorced, got remarried, had another child, and, now, I imagine that he is around six months away from having a good mid-life crisis. I suspect he will buy a sports car, an electric guitar, and jump out of a perfectly good plane, trying desperately to hang onto his dwindling youth. I'll enjoy watching his new adventure. I might even encourage it.

Andrew's brain is sharp, and he can see things that I can't. That's what makes him a successful lawyer.

"What's up?" he asks. "Why have you called me out here?"

"Patrick."

Andrew sighs. "Look, I know the guy is a prick, but he is my friend. He has had my back for my whole life, and I am sure that he will have my back again. He has done a lot for me, and for my family. I know that you don't like him, but I thank you for helping him out. I would help him out, but he said he needed your skills. What's he done this time?"

"He's caught up in some trouble. How much do you know about his past?"

"Most things. There wouldn't be a lot that I don't know about him."

"I am going to share something with you, and I don't want it to be repeated – not to Patrick or to anyone else."

"I understand," my little brother nods his head.

"Patrick witnessed a murder when he was in his early twenties and the person who committed the murder was never found guilty. He removed evidence from the scene of the crime, and has held onto that evidence ever since. That evidence is now missing."

"Who is he protecting?"

"I'll keep that close to my chest."

"That sounds big."

"It is."

We pause our private conversation for a moment to let Dave serve my brother a whiskey.

"What has he hired your services for?" Andrew nods to Dave as he walks away.

"He wants me to find the missing evidence."

"Do you have any leads?"

"I do. I have two leads. A girl named Jessica who works with Patrick's wife at the hospital, and the New Age priest, Tan Do."

"The priest?" Andrew is surprised. "Interesting."

"Andrew, do you know anything about the evidence that he was hiding?"

"Sorry, brother, I have never heard of it. He never mentioned it once to me. What sort of evidence is it?"

"A gun."

"A gun? Why wouldn't he have just thrown that away? Why keep it for two decades?"

"Some sense of protecting the killer, I think."

Andrew nods. "There is no time limit to the statute of limitations for murder; however, there is for manslaughter. For manslaughter, the statute of limitations is five years. If he could prove that it was manslaughter and not murder, then he wouldn't have anything to worry about. It is outside the time frame for the charge. And I'm sure that any good lawyer will be able to argue that it was manslaughter. I can't imagine that after all that time, there would be much evidence to convict him with."

"This is more about protecting reputations than it is defending a criminal offense."

"So you think that the person who stole the evidence was looking for it? Which means they would not have only had to have known about the murder, but they would have had to have known about the evidence."

"That's right. So whoever stole the gun is indeed a dangerous person."

"Where was the gun stored?"

"A small safe."

"A safe?" Andrew says, pausing to think for a few moments. "Maybe they haven't been able to open the safe yet?"

"Possibly. However, I think that the thief is going to hold Patrick to ransom. I think they are going to extort money from him for the evidence. That seems to be the only logical explanation at this point."

"That's heavy," my brother shakes his head. "I've met this priest, Tan Do. I didn't like him. Patrick took me along to one of their church sessions, and it was all singing and dancing and pop music. It wasn't like any church I have ever been to. But I knew something was off with this priest. He looked shifty. And I can tell you, they had a lot of money in that church. Tan Do drove a very nice car."

"What's Patrick connection to the church?"

"They gave him the start as a motivational speaker. He did a few sermons at the church, and Tan Do was impressed with his capacity to reach people. So Tan Do funded his first video and motivational seminar. He was the chief backer of Patrick's operations. Patrick doesn't need any support now, but he splits some of the profits from his exploits back with the church. I think they had a deal that if Patrick made it big, he would share the profits."

"So Tan Do would be unhappy if Patrick would be branching out on his own?"

"Patrick wouldn't do that. He's loyal and-"

"Loyalty is not a word in Patrick's vocabulary," I cut my brother off.

"That's true," Andrew shrugs. "What are your thoughts?"

"I've looked this 'Heaven's Angels' church up online. There's a lot of information about them, and confession is a big part of their church. It is possible that Patrick confessed the murder to Tan Do. That's how he could know about the weapon."

"True."

"And if Patrick has outgrown the church, maybe he is pushing to break free from their original arrangement. Patrick could be trying to push the church out of the picture, and keep all the money for himself."

"And so you think Tan Do has taken the gun as a ransom? A guarantee that Patrick will never cross him?"

"Possibly."

"What do you need from me?" Andrew is always eager to help me.

"Keep your ears open. If you hear anything, let me know straight away."

"Will do," he nods.

We both sit quietly at the bar for a few moments, thinking about the case.

"What do you think she would be doing these days?" I say, not looking up from my whiskey.

"Who?"

"Molly."

Andrew stares at me and then takes a long breath. "Law. Our sister would be putting the bad guys away. That's what she wanted to do. And she would be loving it."

"You're right. She was always the good one," I stare at my drink. "She was always the most morally sound person in the family. Do you remember the day Dad wanted to put a shed in the yard, but he had to chop down a tree to do it?"

"And a family of squirrels lived in the tree," Andrew chuckles. "So Molly wouldn't let him cut it down. Yeah, I remember that. Dad wasn't happy, but he couldn't upset his Molly."

We both smile at the memory from our childhood. It was so long ago, but it is still so fresh in my mind.

"Tom," Andrew says in a solemn tone, "Everyone is guilty of something. I'm sure your sheet isn't clean. Patrick has helped me out in the past, but if you don't want to help him, I understand that. You have no obligation to stay with this case. You can walk away from this one."

"If I wanted to walk away, I would have done it already."

"Then why hold yourself to the case?"

I think for a few long moments before responding. "Curiosity has always been my greatest flaw."

5

Every time I enter a church, I feel a shudder go along my spine, even in a New Age church like this one.

I'm not sure if that is some overarching power trying to tell me something or if it is my body's physical reaction to the place, but it happens every single time.

The feeling might be the result of being forced to attend church every Sunday as a child. When I was six years old, I was sitting in the car when I saw Mr. Mason, the church's best volunteer, stealing two beers from the local store. From that moment forward, I thought there was something strange about watching people praise the Lord on a Sunday and steal from people on a Monday.

That's not to say that church isn't full of great people. It is. Some of the most genuine people I have met in my life have been churchgoers. They will do anything for anyone. But there is always a small number of people willing to make it bad for everyone else.

And when the priest is the worst, then you know that you are barking up the wrong tree.

"Hello, my son," Priest Do greets me as I walk through his church.

"I'm no son of yours," I growl. "We will talk outside of this church. I don't feel comfortable in here."

The New Age church looks more like a large lecture theatre than it does a place of worship. There are two tiers of comfortable leather chairs, all pointing down to the large stage, which is backed by a large projector screen. There are no windows in the large theatre, no symbols of the cross. Instead, there are inspirational posters on each wall, motivating the people do great with their lives.

This certainly isn't the way I remember church. I guess the world has changed.

Priest Do agreed to meet me, but only inside the church. I heard that he does that a lot. He tries to convince people that he is righteous because he is surrounded by posters of faith. The posters don't fool me. I can see straight through his act.

I believe in a God. I don't think that human existence is the result of a perfect set of coincidences, but I don't believe in church. I especially don't believe in one that Priest Do is in charge of.

His fingers are covered in gold rings, his shirt is Polo Ralph Lauren, and his shoes are Salvatore Ferragamo. This man has money.

Tan Do looks at me with belittling eyes. He is Vietnamese born and came to America when he was three years old. Although he looks Vietnamese, his accent is clearly a New Yorker.

"As the Lord would wish," he nods, using a holy voice that is bound to irate me by the end of the conversation. "The Lord is great and we will do as he wishes. If you would like to discuss matters outside these walls, then that is what we will do."

Despite all the trimmings of wealth, what annoys me most is he talks of the greatness of God like it is some badge of honor for him.

"What do you know about Patrick Walker?" I ask as soon as we step out of the dark church doors into the bright sunshine.

"A lot," his answer is strangely suspicious.

"I need more details." I don't ask a question; I make a demand of him.

Tan Do pauses for a while, sighs in a priestly fashion, and then calmly says, "I think everyone should pay for their sins."

"In gold?" I nod towards the rings on his finger.

"No," he shakes his head. "God will judge people, not on what they wear, or what they have bought, but on what they have done in this world. When our judgment day comes, the Lord will judge us. That is the beauty of the afterlife. We will pay for our sins under the decree of the Lord. What you and I do on this Earth will be judged when our day comes."

"And what are your sins?"

"Caring too much," his answer is quick and clearly rehearsed. "I sometimes lose sight of the big picture because I am too focused on making the little things count. I want to help everyone I meet. I want to spread the word of Christ to every individual I meet. However, as much as I worry that I haven't done enough, I know I have done my job. I have made a difference in this world. I have done my best to spread the good news of the Lord Jesus Christ, our Savior."

It sends a chill up my spine when I hear him talk about the Lord.

There is something not real about the way this man speaks.

He feels fake.

For him, this is a job.

It's not a calling, a life's passion, or a call to a higher purpose. No, this man is here because he gets paid well, and he has a lot of power in the community.

"I don't like you," I am blunt as I stare into his eyes. "And I don't like that you deal drugs."

He is shocked by my blunt comment. He is intimidated, and I would feel bad for intimidating a priest, but this man is not your average priest. He is a dodgy criminal.

"I… don't…" he shakes his head.

"I know that you deal drugs. I know that is where a lot of your money comes from. And if I find any evidence of this, I will take you down."

The shock on his face is clear.

"Do you know anything about a safe?"

"I know a lot of safes." Again, he is evasive.

"One in Patrick's house."

He grins. He feels like he is back on the front foot. "I know that one shouldn't keep secrets. It is not right to keep secrets. It is best to be open and honest, especially in front of the eyes of the Lord. If you hold a secret within you, it can destroy you later. Confession can alleviate you of your guilt. You should come to confession one day. I will listen to your sins."

"Stop with lies. I don't like listening to you use the name of the Lord. It feels blasphemous," I growl.

"What do you want?" his voice and expressions change drastically, and it catches me off-guard. Gone is his priestly tone, replaced with a natural sounding New Yorker street accent.

He has let his guard down. He no longer has to act with me. Suddenly, he feels like an average Joe on the street, someone that should be working in an office crunching numbers rather than preaching to the masses.

"Why do you hate Patrick Walker?"

"I don't hate him as such, but I do not want him to walk away from his responsibilities to the church."

"And what responsibilities are those?"

"He donates a lot of money to the church. He is very generous. And that money enables me to spread the good news of the Lord."

"By purchasing expensive cars?"

"Those cars enable me to spread the good news. I need transport."

Without Patrick's donations, the church's income would drop.

And that would affect Tan Do's lifestyle.

It's a good deal.

Tan Do supported him at the beginning, and in return, Patrick donated large amounts of money to the church. I am sure that Tan Do saw Patrick as a business investment rather than someone to help.

It was a good business deal, but not one that I would usually associate with the church. But, this is not just any church, and he is not just any priest.

I came here to put pressure on Tan Do, and to let him know that I am looking into the case.

People make mistakes when they are under pressure. I just need to be watching when Tan Do makes his.

"I'm watching you," I say firmly, and turn around to leave Tan Do behind me.

I will be very happy to take this man down.

6

Kate Jones is a strikingly beautiful woman.

Her eyes are deep blue, her blond hair flows over her tanned shoulders, and her ample bosom is in contrast to her tight waist. Her skin is flawless, her teeth are perfectly white, and her smile melts men with ease. Beauty is a gift given randomly to youth, and Kate has been given the full package.

She is stunning.

But man, this woman eats loudly.

"Remind me to never have a lunch meeting with you again," I mention as she digs into a burger.

"Why not?" she mumbles with a mouth full of food.

"Have you never been told that you are the loudest eater in the world?"

"You know, it's funny that you should say that because just yesterday a waiter asked if I could 'consume my soup a little quieter.'"

"Ha!" I laugh. Any man who messes with this strong woman is either plain stupid or stupidly brave. "And what happened to him?"

"I told him to shove the menu up his ass."

"That's my Kate," I smile. She might look like a model, but this great woman would be more at home on a Texas construction site than a bikini photo-shoot.

"Want to hear a joke?" she says as she slurps a mouth full of sauce off the edge of the burger.

"Is it racist, sexist, or really bad?"

"Don't know," she grins. "I'll tell you the joke, and you can make your own decisions."

"Go on," I nod.

"So Mick and Paddy are sitting at the bar, and Mick turns to Paddy and says, 'Hey Paddy, I'm thinking of buying a dog. I'll think I'll buy a Labrador.' 'Don't do it!' screams Paddy. 'Have you seen how many of their owners go blind?'"

I grin. I'm sure that Kate was a construction worker in a past life.

"What have you got for me, Kate?" I change the conversation.

Kate stops powerfully munching her burger, licks each finger twice, and then reaches into her handbag to pull out a file. "I've got-"

I raise my hand as a stop sign, stopping her from talking any further. She understands and finishes her mouthful of the burger before she continues.

After she takes a massive gulp of food, she starts again. "I've got some information on both Jessica and the priest. We deal with a lot of interesting characters, Tom, but the priest is very juicy. I love it when there is something to look into. This priest shouldn't be a priest, Tom. He has a history of accusations, but, nothing has stuck. Doesn't have a criminal record, either."

"And the girl?"

"The girl, Jessica Watson, is the opposite. She is a true angel. She helps people, Tom. And not just helps the old lady across the street, or donates two dollars to a charity one a month. I mean, this girl really helps people. She is a nurse by day, but, at night, she runs a volunteer center for helping people with mental health issues. She seems to spend all her spare time there. I talked to some of the people walking out of the center, and they couldn't talk highly enough of her. One young girl told me that Jessica Watson saved her life. Jessica gave her someone to talk with, and somewhere to turn when her life was falling apart. The girl talked about suicide, but, Jessica gave her hope. That story touched my heart, and my heart is usually made of stone. Some people are good, Tom, but this girl is practically a saint."

"Doesn't help me."

"She does have a nervous look about her, though. I tailed her yesterday for a couple of hours. Everything she did was filled with nerves. She stopped off at the drug store for a few moments, and it was just long enough for me to take her bag. I took the bag outside, had a look through, and then dropped it off at the counter, saying that I found it outside. She was just coming up to the counter to say that it was stolen. Perfect timing, if I don't say so myself."

Kate is a very skilled woman. She has spent time on both sides of the law – first as a trainee cop, but that didn't last long.

She was caught breaking into the home of a thief that had just been charged. She was trying to steal his television. She explained that it was justice for what the thief did. Kate didn't want to play the role of a cop - she wanted to play the role of karma.

"Good work, Kate. What did you find in the bag?"

"Something very interesting," she smiles. "You'll like this a lot."

"What is it?"

"A picture of Patrick Walker," she says, as she slides the picture across the desk toward me.

"This isn't a new photo," I mention. "It's wrinkled, small, and Patrick looks five years younger."

"It sure is an old photo," Kate says. "But why would she have an old photo of Patrick?"

"Maybe she is holding a grudge against Patrick?"

"What for?"

"You know what Patrick was like as a cop – he was a prick. He might have done something to her that she has never forgotten about."

"Maybe," Kate shrugs, "or maybe she has a massive crush on him. These motivational speakers are almost evangelical to some people. They have a cult-like following amongst the desperate. She might be a massive fan of his, and she may be stalking him."

She is right. The people who follow these motivational speakers can be as crazy as Rolling Stones groupies from the seventies. They will do anything to be close to the speakers.

"And what about the priest?"

"I found out what I expected to find. He was as criminal as they come. He would do anything for money. Word on the street is that he imports drugs from Mexico and sells them to the dealers on the street. He doesn't get his hands too dirty, but he is the importer."

"Anything else?"

"There is a large anonymous donation to the church each week. I tracked that donation, and it appears that it comes from Patrick."

"The photo of Patrick intrigues me, though. We need to chat with her," I say, "but not yet. We have to go to Patrick's apartment now."

"But I haven't finished my burger," Kate complains as I stand to leave.

I turn around to say something, but Kate has already shoved the remaining half of the burger into her mouth.

"I'm… ready… ugh," she mumbles with food dropping out of her mouth.

I sigh and shake my head. "Just finish eating before we get into the car."

7

Patrick Walker's Manhattan apartment is what I would expect from a man who has earned his money from making motivational speeches. The penthouse apartment has a private rooftop garden, four bathrooms, five bedrooms, and a view that most tourists would pay top dollar for. This is a place of pure luxury.

When success hit his bank balance, Patrick moved his wife and children from their modest house in Brooklyn to the expensive Spring St in SoHo. Rumor has it that the apartment previously belonged to a rock legend. The apartment is a testament to Patrick's success on the motivational speaking circuit. It is the validation that he needs to prove to himself that he is successful.

Patrick makes most of his money on the road - he travels to the world's big cities, shouting his formula of success at anybody who is willing to pay for it. He tells people to focus on what they love, teaching them about how to find what they are passionate about. He shouts at the lazy, screams at the unmotivated, and chants at the lethargic.

He has a deep, strong voice, and, backed by uplifting music, it hits a nerve with most people. His YouTube videos were his first hit, then a tour, then a book, and then end-to-end tours. I watched his videos – they are motivating in the same way a personal trainer is in the gym. It's not for me, but I guess it works for some people.

Well, it works for Patrick's bank balance anyway.

Patrick has arranged to meet Kate and me at the door of his apartment because I have told him that I do not want him in there when we are looking around. I need the freedom to think and to wander his apartment without pressure. If there is a clue in there, it will be hidden away, and I won't find it if Patrick is telling me what I can't touch.

Patrick has advised that his wife doesn't know about the safe. The thought crosses my mind that the couple have been together for just under ten years, and yet, she doesn't know about the safe. Either Patrick is determined to keep secrets from her, or she does know and ignores her husband's secrets for the sake of family peace.

But the more I think about it, the more I am sure that this is not the first secret he has kept from her. I am sure that he has many, many secrets, and I think their names would be Ebony, Tiffany, or Hope.

Patrick is nervous when he greets us, uneasy about letting Kate and I wander through his house unwatched.

"You have 30 minutes," he states firmly.

I nod, and Patrick gently opens the door, drops his head, and lets us in. He shuts the door behind us, and I lock it as soon as it closes.

This is our time to sort out these clues.

Inside, his home is everything capitalist dreams are made of. This place could be in the centerfold pages of an up-market catalogue shoot. The appliances are spotless, the children's toys are perfectly placed in a line, and the windows are smudge free.

The well-lit, smiling family photos hanging on the walls look forced, as though his wife is trying to mask any of the pain that must go with living with an ass like Patrick.

"Where to start?" Kate asks.

"Look for anything that might be out of place, Kate."

"I'm afraid we won't find much evidence in here, Jack. It looks like everything has been sprayed with disinfectant."

"You're right," I nod. "This place looks more sterile than a hospital."

"Do people actually live in here?" Kate grimaces. Cleanliness is not one of her strengths.

After scanning the kitchen, lounge, and bedrooms, I walk into Patrick's home office. It is a stark contrast to the rest of the house. Situated in the middle of the third floor, the office has no windows, and it is dark, messy, and isolated.

This is a lonely man's space.

Patrick explained earlier that the safe was stored in the large cupboard in his private office, under a pile of books and shoe boxes. If the thief was looking for the safe, they must have been looking hard.

"Who places a lock on their family office?" Kate questions as she looks at the door.

"Someone who wants to keep secrets from his family."

Slowly, I open up the large wooden cupboard to see it filled with paper files, shoe boxes, and old clothes that could do with some mothballs. The cupboard is more fitting to a college student than a multi-millionaire.

Searching through the pile of old documents, I look for any clue that might help us.

And then I see it.

A small gold bracelet, hanging off a nail in the back of the cupboard wall. It looks like the bracelet fell off when someone was reaching for something in here. I doubt that a former detective would have missed something like this, but with Patrick, he could have missed anything.

Gently, I lift the bracelet off the nail and read the inscription:

Dearest Father Do, May your life be filled with love.

"Well, that it's then," Kate quips from over my shoulder. "Case solved. It was the priest. Let's go and collect the money."

I stare at the bracelet for a while longer.

"But you're not sure," Kate questions my look.

"It's too obvious, Kate. It's too easy. It feels like we are getting played."

"By whom?"

"I'm not sure, Kate, but we are going to find out."

8

Outside the apartment, Patrick is nervously waiting for us.

"Nice pad," Kate quips, as she steps out the door. "It's too clean for me, but I guess some people love to live in places where they can't touch anything."

Patrick takes one look at Kate, and looks back to me with disdain.

It must be hard being Kate. People judge her beauty as a statement that she has no intelligence behind that long, flowing head of blond hair. That's not true. She is one of the most intelligent, street-smart people I know.

Even the best things that life can give you has its drawbacks.

"Kate, I'll meet you in the car," I say, trying to ease Patrick's tension.

"Of course," she grins, and makes her way down the steps.

Patrick stares at the tight butt walk away, which is squeezed into a very tight pair of jeans.

"I hope you didn't make a mess. My wife doesn't know much about this, and she will ask a lot of questions if anything is out of place. And I mean anything. If a coffee cup has moved, then I will have to explain why."

"We didn't touch anything except for what was in your office," I reply.

"Good. She doesn't go in there," Patrick states.

"I can tell."

"So did you find anything in there, Tom?" he questions. "Anything that you can use to push this case along? I don't think I need to remind you that time is very valuable in this case. I need this case to move quickly. I need to find that safe."

"Maybe."

"Maybe? That's all you are going to give me?" Patrick starts to raise his voice.

I take a deep breath, puff my chest out, and take a step closer to Patrick. That move usually defuses any situation. As a tall, strong, dominant man, most people take a step back when I step forward. Attack is the best form of defense.

"Patrick, when was the last time you checked your office?"

"Two days ago," he says, calming his voice. He takes a small step backwards, uncomfortable with my dominance. "After I realized the safe was missing. I haven't been in there since. I didn't want to touch anything."

"Did you search the cupboard?"

"Of course. I'm a former detective, Tom. Of course, I searched the room," Patrick says, rubbing his chin. "But, I didn't find anything. There was nothing left behind. And, it was only the safe that was stolen. Nothing else. No documents, no money, no clothes. Just the safe. They knew what they were looking for."

"I can imagine that in a house like this, security is the top of the range. What security are you running here, Patrick?"

"Motion sensors. Anything that triggers the motion sensors sets off the alarms, and the security company is dialed. They then make the decision whether to call the police or not. I checked; the alarms have been on all the time when we haven't been in the house, and nothing has been triggered."

"So it is not likely that someone broke into the house," I say, and look down to Kate, who is standing beside the car, munching loudly on a bag of crisps. "And who has been in your house since?"

"My wife, the kids… Jessica Watson…" his thoughts tail off. "Of course."

"When?"

"Jessica has been coming past a few times lately. My wife and her are good friends. Jessica is always coming past to share a glass of wine after their shifts at the hospital. You know, I tell my wife that she doesn't have to work anymore, but she won't listen to me. It really pisses me off that she won't stay at home. I mean, why go to work when she has everything she needs here? Man, that really gets under my skin."

I shake my head, and bite my tongue. Now is not the time to get into a discussion about how Patrick treats his wife. Ideally, I would grab the man by the scruff of the neck, slam him against the wall, and tell him how to treat women properly. He hasn't said her name once to me; he only ever refers to her as 'his wife.'

And, of course, if she wants to work, she should work. Valuably adding to the community is a wonderful thing. Patrick could learn a thing or two about that.

"When was the last time Jessica was here?" I question, holding back a rant about his self-focused attitude.

"She came in yesterday when I wasn't here. She came here to talk with my wife about rosters at the hospital, and then my wife left her here to look after the kids for ten minutes while she went out to the shops."

"Was that after you came to my office?"

"Yes… I came to your office yesterday morning. Jessica came around last night while I was still working at my office."

I nod.

"Wait? Is it Jessica? What's going on?"

"Maybe. But I also found this in your cupboard," I hold out the necklace for Patrick to look at.

"Who does that belong to?" he looks at the inscription, but then I take the necklace back.

"If I were you, Patrick, I would have a little chat to your priest friend before things escalate."

9

I love the smell of an old New York City apartment building.

The smell reminds me of my Uncle Toby, who used to live on the tenth floor of a decaying building in Brooklyn. As I grew older, I came to realize that Uncle Toby was a very weird man, but to a child, he was always entertaining. He handed me my first porno magazine at ten years old, passed me my first beer at eleven, and gave me my first driving lesson at twelve. He didn't care about the law. He didn't care about any rules. That is probably why he is currently in prison, serving five years for breaking and entering.

Jessica Watson's apartment building has been forgotten about.

The lift is broken, and by the appearance of the 'Do Not Enter' sign, it is either a frequent occurrence, or the sign has been sitting there for many months.

It's just approaching dinner time, and each floor I walk up brings its own distinct smell. First floor, it's the hit of a strong Indian curry; the next floor, Lebanese, and the next floor is clearly Chinese. By the time I have reached the sixth floor, I could eat a horse.

If you rented an apartment on the sixth floor of this old building, then you wouldn't want to be struggling with your fitness. But, after one week of walking up these stairs, fitness wouldn't be a problem.

After three heavy knocks on the door of apartment 603, I hear the rustling of someone trying to hide something, and then the heavy breathing of someone checking the peephole. By the sound of the anxious breaths, I can tell that this woman is trying to hide something.

The door props open a little, and voice asks, "What do you want?"

"Hello Jessica Watson."

The door opens some more.

"Do I know you?" the blond woman on the other side of the door is small, curvaceous, and looks like she would have fight in her when pushed.

"You don't know me yet, but we are going to become close friends, Miss Watson."

I hold out the necklace I found in the office. Her eyes open wide.

"That's not mine."

"Yes. It is," I reply firmly.

She takes a moment to register my answer.

"Are you a cop?" she asks.

"No."

"What do you want?" she is direct. I like that.

"I want to talk with you."

"I don't want to talk."

"I think you should," I stare at Jessica with intensity, and she stares back for a moment, and then reluctantly opens the door.

I decided to go to this discussion alone, and leave Kate in the office to complete some paperwork. As great as Kate is as an assistant, she has a habit of putting her foot deep into her mouth. That won't help me here.

"Why don't you have a seat and tell me what you want?" Jessica mumbles as she points to the couch. As I turn my back, she moves to the dresser on the right of the room.

"There is no need for the gun, Jessica," I say, without turning around.

It takes her a moment to register my response. Any woman in her situation would be looking for safety, and Jessica is clearly positioning herself nearest to a weapon. That's understandable. I would do the same.

"Are you armed?" she asks.

"Always," I say as I steadily sit on her worn couch. My body sinks into the cushions that must be at least thirty years old. I would say that it hasn't been washed in that long either.

"Then I should be armed as well," Jessica says nervously, as she hovers near the dresser.

I raise both hands as a sign of surrender, and then slowly reach my left hand under my jacket and to my holster. Gently, I remove the gun, release the cartridge, and place it on the coffee table in front of me.

"Is that all you are carrying?" she asks.

"Yes," I reply calmly.

"Ok…" Jessica finally moves away from her dresser, and then comes across to a kitchen stool that sits opposite the couch. "Who are you, and what do you want?"

"My name is Tom Whiskey, and I am a private investigator. I have been hired by Patrick Walker to investigate the disappearance of his safe."

"I have no idea what you are talking about."

I stare at her intently, and she withers under my stare. She first makes eye contact, and then quickly looks to the floor. She's lying.

"This is your father?" I nod towards a picture on the wall. I am trying to build rapport with the young woman to ease her abundance of nerves. Her fingers twitch nervously as she looks at the photos, and her brow is furrowed. My presence is clearly stressing her out.

There are seven pictures on her wall, and six of them have the same older man in it with a young child. I assume Jessica is the young girl in the photos. I chose that as a topic of conversation because I feel that this man would bring a sense of calm to her. She is clearly hero worshipping this man.

"It is my father," she replies with a tinge of sadness. "His name was Timothy Watson."

"He looks happy."

"He was a happy man."

"Was?"

"He died nineteen years ago."

"I'm sorry to hear that," I say softly.

"He died when I was twelve years old. It was the hardest time of my life, and there still isn't a day that goes by that I don't think about him. Every morning I blow a kiss up to heaven, and I know that he is watching over me. I can feel his presence around me when I need him," she says freely.

I nod.

Despite being around death my whole life – first in the Army, and then as a private investigator – it is still the only conversation topic that makes me uncomfortable. I don't know where to look when a person tells me that a loved one has died.

I let the uncomfortable pause linger in the room to show my respect for her loss.

"He's the reason I do a lot of volunteering," Jessica continues. "My father was a great man, but, after my mother died of cancer, he lost his way. In the end, he had a lot of mental problems. I know if someone was there for him, he could have been fine. He ran into a lot of trouble. It didn't end well for him."

"That must have been hard to watch," I say with empathy. "Is that why you do a lot of volunteering?"

Jessica looks at me in surprise.

"I always do a background check on the people I meet," I say, confirming her suspicion.

"It's part of the reason why I volunteer," she says softly. "After my father died, I suffered a lot of anxiety. I still have a problem with it. As a volunteer, I manage a help center for those with mental illness. I'm a trained counselor, as well as a nurse, and I see a lot of people that can't afford help. In the center, we see a lot of middle aged men, and a lot of young girls. I help the middle-aged men because I feel like I am helping my father. And I help the young girls because I feel like I am helping myself."

"That's very honorable."

"It's my passion. It's what I live for. I want to make a difference in the world, and let people know that they are not alone. I spend all my spare time down at the center. There is a young girl who comes in once a week at the moment, and she reminds me a lot of myself. She has lost both her parents, and is struggling to find her place in the world. Her father was murdered, like mine. I sit there and listen to her for hours. I want to help her. I don't want her to suffer the same issues I suffered."

There are tears in Jessica's eyes.

This is clearly what she is passionate about.

But, I am not here to talk about how much good she does in the world, so I bring the conversation back to my case. "How well do you know Priest Tan Do?"

"I don't really know him. I mean, I have met him once or twice, but I didn't really warm to him. I thought he was very arrogant and conceited. He certainly wasn't what I expected from a priest. There was nothing holy about him at all."

"But, you know him well enough to try and set him up?"

"I don't know what you are talking about," she tries to avoid the obvious.

"You left the bracelet in Patrick's cupboard as a diversion. It was a good try. A cop may have fallen for that trick, but not me, Jessica. I saw straight through it."

Jessica leans forward, and pulls her arms into the sides of her chest, squeezing her breasts together. My eyes linger, and she knows it.

"Listen," her tone of voice changes to sound like a sultry telephone sex-worker. "I don't know what you are talking about."

I could see how that tactic would work.

Jessica Watson is a very beautiful woman. Her figure is full, her curves are sexy, and her demeanor is seductive.

And her cleavage is very enticing.

"That won't work on me," I lie. If she keeps it up, I will fall for that seductive routine.

"What will work on you?" she winks.

"The truth," I reply. "I have always been a sucker for the truth."

"You don't care about the truth," Jessica sits back up, and her voice returns to her original tone. "You private investigators only care about money. I know your type. I have met men like you before. All you want is the pay check at the end of the case, and you are happy. You don't care who you step on, or who gets charged. If you really cared about the truth, you would have become a cop. You just want money."

"But, to get the pay check, I need to do my job. Now, Jessica, where is the safe?" I ask firmly.

She pauses before answering. "I sold it."

"Why?"

"Because I couldn't open it," she shrugs. "I couldn't figure out a way into it. It was a lot harder than I expected. I thought I could just google how to break in, and pop, the safe would come open. But I couldn't get into it."

"Who did you sell it to?"

"A guy named Roger Paige. He is connected to the church. I'm sure that Tan Do knows him. You should go and ask him. He's real trouble. I think that Roger Paige may have even bought the safe for Tan Do. He's your man."

I grin. Jessica is trying very hard to push me towards Tan Do. "Why only steal the safe, Jessica? Why break into a house and not steal anything else? There is money in that house, and you and I both know that. But you ignored the money, and went only for the safe. Why would you do that?"

"Because the safe was covered in dust. It was untouched. I figured that I could take that, and get away with it. Nobody would notice a missing safe that hadn't been touched for years, would they?"

"Do you often steal safes, Jessica?"

"This was my first," she nods with a serious look on her face.

"Then why plant the necklace, Jessica? Why try and set-up Tan Do?"

"It was just to blame someone else. That's all I wanted to do. I knew that if something valuable was in that safe, then they will look for clues. It was a diversion. That's all," she says as she brushes her hand across her face.

That is an obvious sign that the person is trying to conceal something. Jessica is lying to me.

I stare at Jessica again. She is avoiding eye contact.

"Tell me, Jessica, what do you think is in the safe?"

"I don't know," she shrugs. "Anyway, I don't have it. I couldn't open it. I imagine that it was something very valuable to Patrick. And Patrick is rich, so if he has something locked away in a safe, it must be worth a fortune. And like I told you, I sold it to a guy named Roger Paige."

"I find it unusual that someone would sneak around the house of a friend, ignoring all the expensive jewelry and money, look deep inside a cupboard within a locked office, and then steal only one thing. I find that very unusual indeed. Actually, I find it so unusual that it becomes very apparent that the person who stole the safe was looking specifically for that safe. And I would like to know why."

"Look, the why doesn't matter. I don't have the safe. I sold it."

I draw a long breath, thinking over my thoughts. Jessica is lying, there is no doubt about that. But she is stubborn, and she won't give me any more information today. I have played my hand, and let her know that I am looking very closely at her.

Jessica isn't a seasoned criminal. She will panic the second I leave this apartment, and she will make a mistake that will lead me to recovering the safe.

"So where can I find this person, Roger Paige?"

"You look like a smart man, Tom. I'm sure you have the skills to find somebody like Roger Paige."

I nod, collect my weapon, and then stand to leave.

"Thank you for your time, Ms. Jessica Watson."

10

Sitting in my black Mercedes, under the shadow of dark tinted windows, I listen to the radio host talk about the dangers of retiring too early. A specialist comes on the radio program and talks about ensuring you have enough funds to enjoy your retired life.

I don't think I could ever retire.

The thought scares me. I'll keep working until my body packs it in, and then I'll sit in an office and run the joint. Despite only being a tick past forty-five, I am beginning to think about the end. If I live to the average life-expectancy for a man in the USA, then I am already halfway through my life.

That thought scares me to hell.

I love a stakeout, but the longer the time ticks past, the more I am left with my own thoughts.

That can never be a good thing.

The car radio hums a tune in the background, and I tap my fingers on the steering wheel. I need to keep my eyes on the building exit. Jessica had panic written all over her face. She is going to try and get rid of that safe before the police show up at her door.

But she can't just walk out with it.

Patiently, I wait for her to leave the building.

After only twenty minutes of sitting in my car, I see Jessica exit her apartment building.

It doesn't look like she is carrying anything big enough to be a safe, but she still looks nervous, checking up and down the street for any signs that she is being followed. Luckily, she doesn't look too hard in my direction.

She hurries along the sidewalk, and down to the subway entrance. If she is going to the subway, that means I have plenty of time before she comes back.

Before I exit my car, I look across the road to the black Lincoln Town Car, parked across the street, four cars back from mine. There is a man sitting in the front, but the windows make it too dark to see who it is.

As I am staring at it, the car drives away.

Being a private investigator means I know the tricks of the trade. I know when and where to look, so if someone is following me, then I will know about it. That car wasn't a coincidence. Someone has a tail on me.

The only tail I am likely to have is from Tan Do, or from Patrick. Neither is a good look. It throws guilt all over them.

Making my way into the apartment building, I spring up the first three flights of stairs, and struggle up the next three.

No wonder Jessica looks fit.

After checking the hallway for witnesses, I put on two leather gloves, and press my body against the door. When I entered her apartment earlier today, I noticed that it was an old key lock that will be easy to bump. One of the skills I developed as a private investigator is breaking and entering, without ever looking like I have broken or entered. A bump key is very good for that.

A bump key is a simple lock picking technique that will open most door locks. I pull out my small set of bump keys, choose the right size, and insert the small key into the lock. By applying pressure, and turning the handle at the right time, the internal mechanics of the door lock will jump up, giving me a split second to turn the handle.

I line the key up, bump the door, and…

Snap.

The door lock pops open.

I am in.

Quietly, I walk into the apartment and close the door behind me, making sure there is no evidence of my forced entry.

I am sure that Jessica has the safe in here.

Her words may have been telling me one thing, but her body language told me the truth.

However, I did believe her when she said she couldn't open the safe.

Scanning the room, I move to the dresser where she was hiding a gun. Looking through the draws, I can't find it. I find a gun box, which indicates it was in here, but no gun. That means Jessica has taken the gun with her.

Interesting.

My visit must have really frightened her.

I check the rooms again for any movement, and unclip my holster. Jessica is now armed, and I have to be prepared for her return.

Without much more thought, I go for the place where any woman would hide a safe - her bedroom clothes cupboard.

Sliding open the doors to the cupboard, I kick back a few layers of shoe boxes, and there it is - the trivial metal gray safe that is paying my wage.

It is exactly like Patrick described it – small, hefty, and dirty.

"I thought you would come back."

I swing around at the voice.

Jessica is standing in the doorway, pointing a gun at me.

"Jessica."

"Tom, you can't have the safe."

"Let's not do anything stupid, Jessica," my right hand goes out to calm her down. I position my body so my left side is obscured from her view. My left hand slowly comes down to my holster. "Just put the gun down, Jessica."

"I've just found a thief inside my apartment. Legally, I can shoot you."

"No, Jessica, you can't. If the police come to this apartment, then they are going to find the safe. And then they are going to ask questions. A lot of questions. You don't want the police asking questions, do you, Jessica?"

She stares at me, the gun shaking in her unsteady hands.

"Did you miss the train, Jessica?" I say with a smile, taking a small step towards her.

"I knew you would come back here. It was obvious that you were going to break in. When I went into the subway, I doubled back and snuck into the apartment building via the fire exit. You didn't think I was just going to let you take the safe, did you?"

"I'm impressed, Jessica. That was very clever," I smile.

"You have to be clever when dealing with criminals like yourself."

"I'm not a criminal."

"You broke in here to steal something."

"Not steal. Just return."

"You can't have the safe, Tom. It doesn't belong to you."

"I see that you haven't opened it yet, Jessica?"

"I haven't figured out a way to do that yet, Tom. Small safes are easy to steal, not so easy to break into. And I can't exactly walk into a locksmith and say 'Hey. I stole this safe. Can you break into it for me?' People get suspicious when you start talking about opening safes. And those people might call the cops. I don't want that."

"So what are you planning to do, Jessica?" I take another step forward.

"I've YouTubed how to open a safe, but so far, nothing has worked. But I'll find a way in."

"I can help you, Jessica," I am deliberately using her name to ease the tension in the room. The quicker I can build the rapport between us, the less likely it is that I will get shot. And I don't feel like getting shot today. "I am very good at breaking into things, Jessica. It is one of my best skills."

She questions me with her eyes. "Why would you do that for me? I'm not paying you. I won't match what Patrick has paid you. I'm sure that I can't afford your fees."

"Curiosity has always been my greatest flaw, Jessica," I say. "And Patrick's case has more than piqued my curiosity. He is very elusive about what is in that safe, and I need to know what is in there."

"It's a gun," Jessica's response is firm and confident.

"How do you know that?"

"Because it is the gun that killed my father."

My mouth hangs open for a moment.

"Your father?" I question, as I try to process what she has just said.

My left hand is now on my gun. If I need to use it, I will.

"Nineteen years ago, my father was shot in a mindless attack in an alley," Jessica says, still holding her gun. "The gun that shot my father is in that safe."

"And how do you know that?"

"Patrick told me."

"Patrick just came out and told you that?"

"Not exactly. Just over a year ago, I was working in a hospital, and Patrick came in for an operation on his shoulder. They assigned me as his nurse. He came to that hospital because his wife works there. She works on the same ward that I do, and she is a real bitch. Anyway, we had to knock him out with gas for the operation. When Patrick was high on gas, he told me all sorts of things – that he cheats on his wife, that he cheats on his poker games with his friends, and that he shot someone in an alley nineteen years ago."

"And from that, you thought it was your father?"

"Once he told me about the murder, I thought that if I could gather enough evidence, I could turn him over to the police. I didn't like him. He treated me like dirt the second he walked into the hospital. I wanted him to go to prison, regardless of who he shot. But, the more questions I asked Patrick about that night, the more apparent it became that he was talking about my father. My father's unsolved murder. He said he still had the weapon in a safe in his home."

"So why not go to the police?"

"I did. They said that people say all sorts of lies when they are high on drugs. They wouldn't even write my enquiry down. They brushed me aside, and said there wasn't enough evidence to reopen the cold case. So I spent a year befriending his bitchy wife, and him, to try and get access to that safe. I babysat those stupid brats so many times, so that I could search his house, his garage, and his rooftop terrace for that safe. Eventually, I found it in his office. I couldn't open it there, so I stole it."

"Then why plant the cross?"

"Because his wife said that Patrick had hired you to investigate missing documents from his office. She told me that there was only one suspect – the priest Tan Do. Renee loves drama, and she took great delight in telling me the story. I rushed out, bought an old cross necklace, had it engraved, and then planted it in the office. It was to throw you off the scent."

I pause for a few long moments.

That was smart, but this woman is not a criminal.

She doesn't have the skills, the knowledge, or the desire to be a thief.

This is a woman full of vengeance – one that wants her father's killer found.

"In that safe is the evidence that proves Patrick is my father's murderer. It was meant to happen like this," she continues. "I need that safe opened, Tom. I'm not letting you leave here with the safe. No way. Not after all the hard work it took to find it."

I take a long, deep breath.

Justice is important to me. It always has been.

It is the reason I do what I do.

I remember as a child, I protected the nerds in the class, because I didn't want the bullies taking their lunch. It was their lunch, and they deserved to have it. As the biggest and strongest kid in class, I had it easy. Nobody would touch my lunch. But it never felt right that someone could take something that wasn't theirs. I wouldn't let it happen.

"I'll open the safe for you, Jessica, but I'll do it for justice."

"Tom, I don't want justice. That time has passed. I want vengeance." There is pain in her eyes. "All those years of knowing that my father's killer was wandering the streets; not charged with his death. That was killing me inside. My father didn't deserve to die on the street. He was a great man, Tom. A great man. And his killer walked free, Tom. That isn't right."

"Justice is important."

"Not justice, Tom. Vengeance."

I stare at her for a long time, before responding. "Put your gun down, Jessica."

Jessica looks off to the side of the room. If I am going to take the gun from her hands, this is my chance.

But I decide against wrestling the gun from her hands.

Eventually, she lowers the weapon.

"Good," I nod. "Put the gun away, Jessica, and let's get into this safe."

Jessica sighs again, and leaves the bedroom to place the gun back into the drawer. I follow her out into the lounge room with the safe tucked under my arm.

"There are two ways into the safe," I comment as I place it on the kitchen bench. "One: we need a heavy duty drill to break through the weak points of the safe. That's the easiest option."

"And where do you get one of those drills?" Jessica asks as she looks over my shoulder.

"I know people who have one. I could leave here and get this safe open by tonight."

"No way. I'm not letting you leave this apartment with the safe. I can't do that. What's option two?"

"I break in," I grin.

"You can do that?"

"When I was a child, my next door neighbor was a retired locksmith. He was always trying to fix some type of lock. People would bring him locks that couldn't be opened – whether it was forgotten combinations, or lost keys, or I suspect, sometimes it was stolen goods. He didn't have any grandchildren of his own, so he enjoyed showing me the tricks of his trade. I learned a lot from that great man; may he rest in peace. I didn't know it then, but those skills have got me a long way in life," I pause to feel the outside of the safe. "Where's the quietest room in your apartment?"

"The bathroom, I guess," Jessica shrugs.

Picking up the safe, I tuck it under my arm again, and walk into the bathroom, with Jessica close behind me. I place the safe on the bench and check that it is an even surface.

"You wouldn't have a stethoscope, would you?" I ask. "That would make this a lot easier."

"I thought that only worked in Hollywood movies?"

"No, it actually works."

"Let me check my old nurses kit. I might have one in there."

Within a minute, Jessica has returned with the stethoscope. "I never even knew I had this."

"Good," I say, as I tap the end of the stethoscope. "Close the door behind you. I need the room to be as silent as possible."

"Ok," Jessica closes the bathroom door.

"I am going to call out numbers, and I need you to write those numbers down on a piece of paper. Jessica, I have to warn you that this is a long process; it's not like the movies. This is going to take some time."

Jessica nods.

Placing the end of the stethoscope against the safe, I listen to the turn of the dial. Firstly, I listen to the number of clicks that happen while I turn the wheel.

"Three," I call out to Jessica.

"Is that the first number?" she asks eagerly.

"No," I reply without taking my focus away from the safe. "That is the number of combinations in the lock."

I spin the dial to reset the position, and then begin to turn the dial slowly, listening carefully for any sounds. When I hear two clicks close together, I call out the corresponding number to Jessica.

"Fifteen," I say quietly.

"Is that the first number?"

I shake my head.

"Five," I call out.

Jessica writes the number down without question.

"Twelve."

"Is that the combination?" Jessica questions again.

"I wish it was that easy," I reply.

I continue calling out numbers for the next fifteen minutes, and Jessica diligently takes notes.

"Eight," I say finally, removing the stethoscope and taking the pen and paper from her hand. I study the numbers, and convert the numbers into two separate graphs.

"What are you doing now?" she asks.

"Studying the left and right contact points for the dial." I analyze the numbers for some time until the formula becomes apparent to me. "Good. We have the three numbers."

"Really?" Jessica is surprised.

"Yes," I grin.

"Well, they do it a lot faster in the movies," she says, cheekily.

I smile, spinning the dial to the numbers I have written down, and…

Snap!

The safe door opens.

We are in.

"Wow…" Jessica is in shock.

She draws a deep breath as I slowly open the safe door.

And, sitting on the bottom of the safe, is a handgun.

I grab a nearby tissue and hold the gun by the end of the barrel, "This is it, Jessica. The piece of evidence that will find your father's killer."

Jessica has tears in her eyes.

"I need a plastic bag to put the gun in," I state. "Don't touch this gun, Jessica. We don't want to smudge the existing fingerprints."

Jessica pulls open the bathroom cupboard and grabs a clear plastic bag. Gently, I place the gun in.

"There is your vengeance," I say, nodding to Jessica.

Her face is pale. After nineteen years of anguish, the realization that she has caught her father's killer hits hard.

"Just be wary that there may be someone else to blame," I say. "Patrick told me that it was his father that shot the man in the alley that night."

"You knew what was in the safe?" Jessica is surprised.

"I knew what was in there, Jessica, but I didn't know that it was related to your father's case."

Jessica stares at the gun for a long time. "This is it. This is the moment that changes everything. This is the evidence that I have wanted to find for nineteen years. This proves that Patrick was my father's killer."

"This might not be enough, Jessica," I warn her. "The justice system isn't as perfect as you think it is. This evidence may not be enough to convict your father's killer."

"It proves it to me. Patrick told me these stories when he was high on gas, so I wasn't one-hundred percent sure that they were true. I didn't know if it was all a coincidence. There was a lot of doubt in my mind that he was telling the truth. But this proves it, Tom. This proves that he was telling the truth. He killed my father, Tom. The contents of this safe proves it."

A long silence falls over the room.

Eventually, Jessica wipes the tears from her eyes, and looks back to the safe.

"What else is in there?" Jessica says, as she pushes the safe door open wide and looks inside. "There is a small box on the shelf. This looks interesting." She gently reaches into the safe and removes the small gift box. Lifting the lid off of the blue, decorated box, Jessica makes a confused face. "Just some old love letters."

Handing them across to me, I immediately recognize the handwriting.

"Old love letters…" This time, the tears well up in my eyes. "To Patrick…"

My world is spinning.

The memories fill my mind, taking me to another place.

"What's wrong, Tom?" Jessica's voice shocks me back to reality.

"These love letters. They are from my sister to Patrick. He must have kept her old love letters," I sit on the titled bathroom floor, leaning against the cupboard, my hand running through my hair as I read the letters.

Wow.

All the letters end the same:

It's just not working out…

I'm sorry, but we can't be together…

We can't fight this. I don't love you anymore…

"She was breaking up with him," I say after I read the third letter. "My sister was breaking up with Patrick."

"Are they still together today?" Jessica asks innocently.

"She died twenty years ago," I say, not taking my eyes off the page. "She was only twenty years old, and dating Patrick, and then she committed suicide. They said that she hung herself. That was the most heart-wrenching experience of my life."

Once I have finished reading the third letter, I stare out at nothing.

The tone of the letter brings back many memories of my perfect sister - her radiant smile, her beautiful blond hair, and her importance in my life. She was my little sister, and I was supposed to protect her.

But nothing can bring her back.

My sister died twenty years ago because of my neglect. I should have been there for her.

All the emotions about her come flooding back.

In a daze, I read the second letter again. One section captures my attention:

I love you, Patrick, but I am not in love with you. Our lives are going separate ways. I know that you want me to be the perfect housewife and stay at home to raise our future children, but the truth is, working is part of my DNA. I have to work. I will not give that up for any man.

I know that you think we are still together, but we are not. We are no longer in a relationship. It is time for you to accept that and leave me alone.

The letter is dated May 14th, two days before my sister's death.

Maybe this is what pushed her over the edge? Maybe the stress of this breakup was too much for her to handle? Maybe the weight of the world was too much for her?

This is the first time I have heard that she was breaking up with Patrick. Nobody knew that. If only she had reached out for help. I could have helped her. I could have listened to her.

Jessica steps over my feet, and looks back inside the safe. "There is nothing else in here except another note, and an old necklace."

She pulls the necklace from the safe, dangling it from her finger. "It's a nice necklace. Maybe it's a family heirloom?"

My world freezes as I lay eyes on the necklace.

"You recognize this necklace?"

"That's my sister's necklace," I say slowly. "I gave it to her the night she died."

11

Time stops as I stare at the necklace.

That's my sister's necklace.

Twenty years ago, I hung that around her neck and kissed her on the forehead for the last time.

She loved the necklace. Her eyes glowed as she talked about the future. She looked so happy.

Slowly, I stand up and take the necklace from Jessica's hand. As I feel the gold lace, the memories overwhelm me. That night, Molly looked like an angel from heaven. Her smile was so beautiful.

"What does that mean?" Jessica questions quietly as I stare intensely at the necklace.

Her words barely sink into my head. Shock has taken over.

Desperately, I return to the love letters that my sister wrote. One is dated the night before she died.

I scan the page until I get to the last line:

We are not right for each other. It has been fun, but I think our lives are going to take different paths. We are not together anymore. I can't handle your anger. I won't tell anyone that you hit me last night, but please Patrick, leave me alone.

Patrick.

Patrick Walker.

He murdered my sister.

She didn't commit suicide. He murdered her.

Patrick Walker murdered my sister.

I have helped that man. I have stood by him in times of need. I stood next to him at my sister's funeral.

My sister's killer has been next to me the whole time.

It all makes sense.

"He killed her," the words tumble out of my mouth.

"Who?"

"My sister. Patrick killed her. Patrick Walker killed my sister. He was with her the night she died. The necklace proves it. I gave this necklace to Molly only two hours before she died. There is no way she would have given it to him and then committed suicide. No way. I never believed that she hung herself. I knew that she wouldn't have done that. Patrick Walker killed my sister."

Standing in the bathroom, I stare at my own reflection in the mirror. The fury fills every ounce of my body. My muscles clench, and my hands grip the basin tightly.

He killed my sister.

I cannot let him get away with that.

"What are you going to do, Tom?"

"I let her down once; I am not going to do it again."

With a heart full of rage, I reach for the closed bathroom door.

"Where are you going?" Jessica questions.

"I'm going to find justice. I am going to find Patrick Walker."

I swing open the bathroom door, and find a gun pointed at my chest.

"Well, Tom, you don't have to go far to find me."

12

"You killed her."

My statement is blunt. I don't care that he has a gun pointed at my chest.

He doesn't respond.

"Why, Patrick? Because she was going to dump you? Is that it? If you couldn't have her, nobody could?"

"What are you talking about?" he asks. He looks confused.

"The love letters from my sister. The necklace that I gave her the night she died. I know you killed her."

"The love letters?" he questions, and I can see the thoughts crash through his head. "They were in the safe?"

"And the necklace."

His mouth drops open. His shock is as clear as mine.

Staring at me, he doesn't know what to say.

"Tom…"

"Don't say anything."

"Tom. I didn't kill her. She committed suicide."

"I gave her that necklace two hours before she died, Patrick. She was happy. She was full of life. The police said that I was the last one to see her alive. Now, I know that is not true."

"Look…" Patrick takes a long pause before he finally responds, "I didn't know that the letters were in the safe. I thought they were in an old shoe box. I hadn't looked in that safe for more than a decade. I didn't realize that the necklace was in there."

"What?" I stare at him. I want to rip his throat out. "You think you're explaining a mistake?"

"Don't make me shoot you, Tom." Patrick nods down at the gun. "I will shoot you."

He is too far away for me to lunge at him and rip the gun away from his hands. I just need to be one step closer…

"Don't take another step," Patrick steps backward as I step forward. "Or I will shoot you."

I need to be within a range of ten feet. If I am within that range, I can lunge to the side of the man and force the gun away from me. I am big enough and strong enough to overpower him. That's what years of training in the Army does for my thinking.

Most situations are sized up within seconds.

Despite the rage pumping through me, I know that he is too far away. I can't grab him from here.

If I lunged, he could kill me. Letting rage take hold of me now would be suicide.

"How long have you been in my apartment?" Jessica questions from behind me.

Realizing that she is concealed behind my body, Patrick nods for her to exit into the lounge room. Jessica holds her hands up like she is in a Hollywood film, but I keep my hands by my side, close to my weapon.

"I am going to take your gun, Tom," Patrick nods towards my belt. "Slowly."

With my eyes fixated on my sister's murderer, he slowly removes the weapon from my belt.

I look for a chance to jump him, but the gun doesn't move from my torso.

Patrick is a former cop, and he has been in this situation many times before. He is calm as he holds the gun on my movements. Gently, he places my gun on the coffee table in the lounge room.

"I followed Tom here," he answers Jessica's question without taking his eyes off me. "I figured that after you left the apartment, if Tom came back in, then he would be expecting to find the safe."

"You didn't trust him?" she questions sarcastically.

"No. I didn't trust Tom. He is too righteous for me. His morals are too high. I only turned to him, because he was the only option I had. There were no other options."

"You killed my sister," I growl through my teeth.

"I didn't mean to, Tom," he snaps. "It was an accident. I got angry when she dumped me, and so I choked her with a rope. That was an accident that I have lived with for a very long time. I loved her. I loved her, Tom. More than anything. It was an accident. That mistake has tortured me for years."

"Tortured you?!" I growl. "She was my sister."

"Nobody would have believed me if I told the truth, Tom. I set it up to look like she hung herself so that I didn't have to go to prison. It was an accident, and I was truly sorry about that, but she was dumping me, Tom. She was leaving me. Molly was the love of my life, and she was walking away from me."

"You bastard." The anger continues to build within me. I can't let him walk away from this. It would be letting my sister down again.

I can't do that.

But I also know that attacking him right now would still be madness.

The years of Army training drown out my need to rip him apart.

"And my father," Jessica adds. "You killed my father."

"Your father?" Patrick questions with a confused look on his face.

"Nineteen years ago, a man was shot in an alley. That man's name was Timothy Watson. He was my father."

"Wow," the shock covers Patrick's face again. "That's quite a development."

"You killed my father," Jessica accuses him again.

"That's why you stole the safe," he says, laughing at the coincidence of the moment. "Who would have thought?" He shakes his head. "But how could you have possibly known what was in the safe?"

"You told me."

"What?"

"You told me when you were high on drugs after your shoulder operation. I was your nurse, and you were telling me all sorts of things. You told me that you cheated on your wife. You told me that you cheat at poker, and then you told me that you shot someone. I thought it was just a story, but the more you told me about that night, the more it became obvious that you shot my father. The man in the alley was my father."

"Wow," Patrick chuckles again. This is all very funny to him. "This is quite the development. Remind me not to take the gas again. Who knows what I will say next time I have an operation? I might even let it slip that I shot two people in this apartment."

His eyes turn sinister.

"You told me it was your father who used the gun, not you," I state. It is important that I keep him talking. If he stops talking, then he has a chance to think. That is not good in this situation.

"I lied to you, Tom," Patrick shrugs again, like it means nothing. "I made up the story about my father to convince you to take on the case. You would never have taken on the case if I told you the truth. Your morals are too high for that. Even though you deal with the scum of the Earth, you are still quite righteous. Not me. I don't have a very high level of morals."

My narrow vision is starting to expand again. My anger isn't as pumping as much as it was. I can see things more clearly now.

"How many others?"

"That I have killed?"

"Yes."

"I don't know," he shrugs. "A few, I suppose."

"A few?"

"There were some that were killed in the line of duty, and there were others that were accidents. I guess around ten to fifteen, but hey, who's counting?" Patrick laughs again. "Your sister was the first."

"You bastard," I growl. "How could you be that person? Your father is such a good man."

"How could I not?" he snaps again. "All my father ever did was give himself to other people. He sacrificed himself for others – that's not honorable. No. That's selfish. He wasn't there for me. He was never there for me. I was nothing in his world. Nothing. He was there for everyone else, but not his family. Not for me."

"He does good in the world."

"Not my world."

The rage boils inside me again. There is too much anger in me to keep him talking.

A pause hangs over the room as Patrick starts to think about his next steps. "Well, it seems we have ourselves a bit of a dilemma, don't we? It seems that we are stuck in this situation with no real way out. Of course, I can't let either of you go; you both know too much."

"What are you going to do?" Jessica is panicked. This is probably the first time she has been held at gunpoint.

Not me.

It is almost a monthly occurrence for my profession.

"You can't shoot me, Patrick," I state firmly. "If you shoot me then the police will investigate my death, and that will lead them to the last case I was working on. Those files will be made public."

"You're buffing. There are no notes. I told you not to make any notes." Patrick is beginning to let his guard down. He is falling into the trap of conversation. I creep half a step closer as he speaks.

"Do you really think I would adhere to that request? Do you really think that I would listen to what you have to say about that? This is my business, Patrick, and I need to have fallback plans." I step closer as I talk. "There are notes. Detailed notes. And my assistant Kate knows everything there is to know about this case."

The gap between us is shrinking.

"What do you suggest then, Tom? How should I deal with this situation?"

"By letting me go," I creep closer.

"Ha!" Patrick laughs again. His guard is down now. "I just admitted that I killed your beloved sister, Tom. I doubt you are going to forget about that."

"If I kill you, then I spend the rest of my days behind bars," I creep closer still.

"Maybe. But I don't think that will stop you."

Closer.

"I think it will."

"You're an interesting man, Tom."

"How so?"

Closer.

"You're-"

WHACK!

My right arm swings, pushing the gun away from my direction. As the gun moves away, my left fist powers towards Patrick's face.

SMASH!

One clean punch to the chin, and he falls like a sack of potatoes.

He is out cold.

13

Standing over my brother's best man, I kick the gun away from his hand. It slides across the floor to the bathroom door.

I stare at Patrick, and all I want to do is rip him apart. This man stood next to my family at my sister's funeral. He stood there after he killed my sister. He lied every day for the past twenty years.

He is a family friend.

And my sister's killer.

"Step away from him, Tom."

My head swings up, and I see Jessica standing at the bathroom door, pointing Patrick's gun at me. I stare at her for a few long moments, but I don't move.

"Tom, I said, step away from him."

"Jessica," I say slowly. "What are you doing?" I slow my speech pattern down to calm Jessica and prevent her from doing anything stupid.

"That prick is mine."

"Jessica, don't do anything rash. You don't want this situation to become worst than it already is."

"No, Tom. That man killed my father, and got away with it for nineteen years. I am not going to let him get away with it again. He is a serial killer. You heard him. He has murdered a lot of people. He needs to pay."

"Jessica, listen to me," I say slowly. "The courts need to deal with this. That is justice. Killing him isn't justice. It is revenge."

"Don't tell me that you don't want to kill him. I can see it in your eyes, Tom. I know that you want to kill him. He killed your sister."

"I want to kill him, Jessica. Every ounce of my body wants to kill him. I want to rip him limb from limb. But that is not justice. That is cheap revenge. Trust me, I am going to beat him within an inch of his life, but then I will let the courts make their decision. He will go to prison. There is enough evidence here to send him away for the rest of his life. And they don't like cops in prison."

"Sorry, Tom. Step away from him."

"Jessica," I say slowly. "Don't do anything stupid. If you shoot Patrick now, then you won't be able to help anyone else. There are people that need an angel like you, and you can't help them from behind bars."

"Don't you get it, Tom?" she says, tears in her eyes. "He is the reason I have lived a life full of anxiety. He is the reason I have lived a life full of pain. He has to pay for that."

"Think about the people that need your help, Jessica. People need you. Imagine if there was someone there for you when you needed it. Someone that could have helped you. If you do this, then there will be nobody there for the people that need it."

"He has to pay, Tom."

"No, Jessica. This is not the right choice."

I see Patrick start to stir out of the corner of my eye. He is on the ground, and his head moves slightly.

"Tom, move back," she points the gun at me.

"Jessica..."

Bang.

14

The sound of the gunshot deafens me.

The world is a blur.

It takes my mind a moment to understand what has happened.

Jessica is on the floor.

Patrick is holding a smoking gun.

My gun.

Patrick looks at me with menace, my gun pointing at me.

"Jessica," I call out.

There is no response.

She is lying on the ground; blood splattered on the wall behind where she stood. Finally, she whimpers softly.

She isn't dead.

Yet.

"Don't move," Patrick stops me before I can move to Jessica's assistance.

"I have to help her, Patrick," I state firmly. "She has been shot."

"Sorry Tom, but that is not going to happen. After that gunshot, the police will be here in a few moments. And by that time, I only want them to hear one story. My story. And it will be the story about how both of you died."

The barrel of my own gun is staring me in the face.

His hand isn't shivering. It isn't wavering.

It is steady.

That is a bad sign.

"Patrick, you can't get away with this," my voice is firm and dominating. I cannot show any sign of weakness to him. "If you shoot me, then you will go to prison."

"Even in the face of your own death, you are still so confident," Patrick chuckles.

He moves to stand up.

This is my chance.

In the spilt-second that he turns to look at Jessica, I lunge forward.

I grab the arm holding my gun.

WHACK!

One punch to Patrick's cheekbone. But it's not enough.

He falters, but he swings back at me with the butt of the gun.

My arm stops the swing, grabbing his wrist.

The gun is point upwards.

It is a battle of strength.

SMACK!

My head lunges forward into his nose.

His grip on the gun is broken.

In one move, I snatch the gun from his hand.

SMASH!

My right fist connects with his nose again. I leap back to standing.

Patrick is holding his bloodied nose, looking at me in fear. I hold the gun towards his head.

"This is the end, Patrick."

There is a moment of reflection between us.

"Do it," he dares me. "Shoot me, Tom. Shoot me."

"No," I shake my head. "Prison is the best place for you, Patrick. They don't like cops in prison, especially not crooked ones."

"You're just going to let your sister's killer go? Shoot me, Tom."

WHACK!

I lunge my right hand into his face, and I feel his nose break under my force.

That feels good.

So, so good.

Having spent a lot of my youth in a boxing gym, I know that if I want to knock someone out, I hit them on the chin.

But, if I want to cause them immense pain, I hit them on the nose.

"Agghhh," he says as he grips his nose, curling up into a ball on the ground.

"I'm not going to kill you today, Patrick. Karma will be your justice."

"Do it," he looks back up at me with a bloodied face. "Do it, Tom. I deserve it."

"Faced with the choice between justice and vengeance, I choose justice."

"I killed her. Your sister, Tom. I killed her," he says through his teeth, blooding dripping from his jaw. "And I enjoyed it."

"Patrick, I choose justice," I say to him. "Justice is coming to you."

Bang.

Bang. Bang.

Patrick's eyes look at me with unhindered fear.

A fast flow of red fills his white shirt.

My head swings around.

Jessica.

She picked up Patrick's gun, and shot him with it.

Patrick's head falls to the floor before he is able to say another word.

The metallic smell of blood fills the room.

"Jessica…" I fall next to Patrick on the floor, holding the wounds of his chest. I check for a pulse. "Jessica, you killed him."

"You may have chosen justice, Tom," she says. "But I chose vengeance."

Epilogue

The taste of a Pappy Van Winkle Family Reserve bourbon whiskey is like heaven in my mouth. It has a smooth wooden finish, filling my mouth with the taste of oak.

This expensive bourbon is the best way for me to debrief from a case.

I always have one glass of this rare and limited whiskey when a job is finished. It is the only time I drink it.

It is a celebration of a completed case, but it is also a signal to my body to let go. The distinctive smell, the unique flavor, and the feeling I get when it washes through my body, is a trigger for my mind to release any feelings I have about the case.

It is a simple psychological trigger that works every time.

In my line of work, it is important to let go.

Not just for the ability to focus on the next case, but also for my sanity.

"Will she go to prison?" Kate questions as she sips her Gin and Tonic.

"No. It was self-defense. Jessica was justified in using that level of force with Patrick," I stare into my drink. "Patrick had told her that he was going to kill her, and had already attempted to do so. She was shot in the shoulder; that was enough evidence for the threat to her life."

Kate shakes her head. "I think she was always going to shoot Patrick. I think once she found the evidence, she was going to have her revenge. Whether it was in her apartment, or in a park late at night, she was going to kill him."

"Maybe. But, we'll never know."

"She could have retreated," Kate says. "It's not self-defense if she had the opportunity to retreat. There is no 'stand your ground' defense in New York, Tom. She could have run away."

"But, the home is the castle, Kate," I sit up straight and look at her. "The duty to retreat does not apply when you are in your own home. Patrick clearly came to Jessica's apartment with the intention of shooting her. She is able to walk away with a clear record."

We are sharing a drink at my favorite bar in New York; Joe's Whiskey Tavern on Tenth Avenue. It is a quiet bar with low humming background music that soothes the soul. I can never take Kate to a busy bar. I made that mistake once, and she spent the entire time rejecting the advances of many men, and some women.

"What will Jessica do now?"

"She'll go back to helping people. Changing lives. Jessica Watson will make the world a better place through her volunteering. That is honorable work," I take a long, deep breath. "Jessica blamed her father's killer for all her anxiety, and all her pain. She wasn't interested in justice for that. She just wanted revenge."

"It's strange that someone can be so good, and yet, so evil."

"Good and evil isn't black and white, Kate."

When I heard that there were no charges against Jessica for Patrick's death, I went to the mental health center where she volunteers. I was going to tell her that she made the wrong choice, but, I walked into the center, and saw her in a meeting room. Jessica Watson was holding a young teenage girl in a tight, warm hug. Their embrace was full of emotion. It struck me that for all of Jessica's pain, something good has come out of it.

Helping others is always the right choice.

"And the priest?" Kate asks.

"It turns out that Patrick had records of all his interactions with Tan Do. He was secretly recording all their conversations, just in case Tan Do tried to blackmail him. The police found all the recordings on Patrick's laptop. Tan Do had talked freely about where he was dealing drugs, who he was importing from, and how much money he was spending on it. Patrick had set Tan Do up as a fallback to the possible blackmail."

"So the priest is going to prison?"

"He is going to prison for a very long time," I smile. "There is no more church for that man."

Kate pauses before she asks the next question. I can tell that she wants to ask another question, but she is hesitant to go ahead. "Come on, Kate. Ask the question."

"Ok," she takes another long pause. "What about Molly?"

I sigh again, and look back to my whiskey. "My brother is pushing for her death recording to be changed from suicide to murder. But in reality, nothing changes," I take another long sip of whiskey. "Nothing will bring her back."

"Tom, do you think Patrick's death is justice?"

"For Molly; yes."

"And for Jessica?"

"I'm not sure," I say, as I take a final sip of whiskey. "But, I have a feeling our paths will cross again…"

<u>END</u>

AUTHOR'S NOTE:

Thank you for reading the first story in the Tom Whiskey series.

This plot had been swimming around in my head for a while, and I finally put it to paper after a year of thinking about it. The main aim of all my stories is to entertain, but, I also wanted to highlight that the line between good and evil can be as gray as an Irish winter.

The character of Jessica Watson is based on a woman I first met while traveling through Ireland. She spent a lot of time helping others, making the world a better place, but, in a moment of madness, she did something wrong. In the end, she was convicted of a crime. However, she continued to spend her time volunteering. Her dedication to assisting other people through their pain has always held my admiration. Despite her one moment of malice, she is a great woman.

I have started writing the next in the Tom Whiskey series, so keep an eye out for it.

Regards,

Peter

ABOUT THE AUTHOR:

Peter O'Mahoney is the author of the Max Harrison and Bill Harvey thrillers.

O'Mahoney was raised on a healthy dose of Perry Mason stories. The pace, intrigue, and style of these books inspired him to write his own set of best-selling legal dramas.

Having majored in psychology, O'Mahoney delves into the thoughts of his characters to find the motivation behind their actions. He loves to blur the line between good and evil.

Writing under various pen names, including children's books under the pen name Peter Patrick, O'Mahoney has entertained hundreds of thousands of readers around the world.

Also by Peter O'Mahoney

The Bill Harvey Legal Thriller Series:

Will of Justice

The Max Harrison Legal Thriller Series

with Patrick Graham:

Criminal Justice

Defending the Innocent

The Paid Juror

Burning Justice

The Girl on the Road

Made in the USA
Columbia, SC
22 April 2024

34756796R00086